Back in the Game

By: James Lewis

James E. Lewi

This book is dedicated to

Captain Brad Hettinger and his family;

Billie, Collin and Courtney,

victims of war and PTSD.

*"May God grant those of us who have born
the battle, the ability of our mind to forget
what our eyes have seen."*

Back in the Game

ISBN 9781719175869

Praise for *Back in the Game*

Lewis' book gives a behind-the-scenes look at the inner working of a police department while keeping the story delightfully entertaining. With years of police work under his belt, Lewis brings realism to his characters, like the homeless winos; Maggie, Big Charlie and Seven Eleven. And I can assure you that once you meet the "Colonel", you'll want to see more of him in future books. Lewis has an acerbic wit that serves him well in the underworld of crime. I highly recommend this book.

Linda Loegel, author of *Saving Lou*

****

Suspense, humor, and memorable characters, *Back in the Game* has it all. Retired Detective Lewis gives us a fly-on-the-wall, entertaining view of detective work that could only be written by someone who has been there. This book will leave you wanting to read the sequel. I loved it!

Nancy Panko, author of award-winning novel *Guiding Missal*

*****

Lewis brings you on a ride-along through the streets and squad room with a riveting plot and an array of unique characters. This tightly woven tale is laced with a mix of twists, jurisdictional bantering, and snappy witticism from top cops to the dumpster burger set. Join ex-wino, the "Colonel"; ex-working girl, Mary; The Kid, aspiring to ex-rookie; and supposed-to-be-retired detective Ray Conway, as he gets *Back in the Game*

Barbara Bennett, author of *Anchored Nowhere; A Navy Wife's Story*

Acknowledgments

To my wife, Marilyn, for her patience and encouragement and apologies for the countless number of times she had to hear and edit the same chapter over again.

To the Cary Alliance Writers Circle, real writers who let me hang around and learn from their knowledge; Ellen, Nancy, Janet, Joanne, Terry, Barbara, Linda, Mac and Harry (RIP).

To family and friends who put up with the questions, "What do you think?" and "Does this sound right to you?"

To my sister-in-law, Brenda Gaines, who read the whole story one chapter at a time and helped me form the Colonel into a real hero.

To my sister, Denise Fauver, who has always been there to encourage me in my adventures.

To Erin McDaniel for spending time with me designing the image of my book cover and then photographing it for me.

To the homeless I met along the way who made this story possible.

To the great men and women I worked with from the federal government and shared many laughs with over a beer when the job was done, and we were safe once again.

To the police who put it on the line everyday, for people they don't know.

Prologue

Plodding downstairs to the kitchen I turn on the news, start coffee, measure out the morning's oatmeal and run water in the sink to wash dishes from snacks the night before. Local television stations, congested with news about the First Lady coming to town, make me glad I'm retired.

Stopping at the sink, I glance at the desk plate reading 'Detective Ray Conway' on the counter, next to the clock they gave me at my retirement party. Retired for months now and I'm still trying to bring myself to put these last few things in a box. Those poor officers out there will be working long hours this week and this time I'm hoping to watch from afar.

After I get Maureen off to work I make the bed, pick up around the condo and throw a load of clothes in the washer before leaving for the gym. With coffee in hand, I cross the street and saunter on down the block to the YMCA and up the steps to the fourth floor, where the next half an hour is spent doing more visiting than working out. The yuppies finally take off to the land of *'Look at me and my importance'*, leaving the flower children and the warriors of the past in control. Treadmills fill up with dirty old men talking about the news, the sports and the cute little behinds of the college girls working there.

Once my coffee is gone and I've been seen by everyone, I head back down the steps and turn in the direction of the coffee shop at Second and Jefferson Streets. Armed now with a second cup of coffee, the bus stop bench beckons and I hunker down, leaning back against the dirty worn plexiglass.

Glancing across the street, the new Hampton Inn looms large, encased in orange brick and reflective glass. People were coming and going through glass revolving doors in the middle of the day on a busy street that would have been empty until the streetlights came on, only twenty years ago. Closing my eyes, the memories come in crisp and clear. The long-gone Marquee Lounge once sat in that same spot. It was an old brown brick building sporting a white wood front, and a red marquee hanging over the sidewalk trimmed with bright lights and housing twelve-inch black letters boasting, 'Girls, Girls, Girls'.

****

While I sat dreaming of the past in Louisville, a Secret Service agent was exiting a car at the Ronald Reagan Airport to begin a trip that would change several lives, including mine. Checking his suitcase and with only a carry-on in hand, he heads to the security office where he persuades a security officer to escort him and his handgun to the plane. There, he meets the pilot and shows him his credentials, making the crew aware of his presence. A male flight attendant seats him before the other passengers board and Agent Joseph Martin quietly surveys his fellow passengers as they begin to pass. Out of habit resulting from several years of police work, he profiles each person. As the plane moves from the gate to start its two-hour trip to Kentucky, Martin opens his case, pulls out a yellow legal pad and starts making notes. He'll need to hit the ground running.

****

The Colonel

Sprawled on the Jefferson Street bus stop bench, I'm lost in yesterday, picturing a long time past at The Marquee Lounge. At that time, it was one of two movie theaters on the downtown Louisville block that showed x-rated films and offered a visual thrill of lightly clad hostesses who made the gentlemen feel quite welcome. The seasoned hostess at the front desk had two jobs; taking the tips the men gave the girls for their company and meeting the police when a customer with no money became handsey with one of her girls. Well, make that three jobs if you count, (*well you know what I mean*). When the police were called, they'd inevitably get a story that would manage to get the customer put out, but not arrested. The manager didn't want the customer arrested, which wasn't good for business, and of course he didn't want his girls arrested either. I'm aware that when I open my eyes, I'll still see the new hotel coffee shop that replaced twenty years of stories, memories and history with one swing of the wrecking ball.

Sensing someone sit down near me on the bench and so as to not lose my dream, I only open one eye to acknowledge their presence. A tall thin black man in his sixties, with the dirt of the street embedded in his clothes, sits down tiredly. Sad eyes framed with heavy wrinkles are a sure sign he has many stories to tell from the troubled miles he's traveled.

"Say mister, you got some change for a coffee?"

Knowing there are more than half a dozen shelters within a stone's throw that served three meals a day and kept a pot of coffee on, I suspect the money was for something with a little more bite. But feeling the need to show this man some respect, I answer, "Looks like you need something a little stronger than coffee, pal. Let's start with a cup and maybe work up to some lunch."

After crossing Jefferson Street in the middle of the block, we enter the hotel lobby under the wary glances of the patrons checking in and out. Turning left in the direction of the coffee shop, I notice the reluctance on the face of the old man. Placing my hand on his shoulder I say loud enough for the people around to hear, "Colonel, I think we've got time for a Starbucks coffee before the meeting." The old man looks up at me and grins, each step becoming more confident.

Entering the coffee shop, we walk confidently up to the counter to place our order. Peering from behind an enormous stack of books, a young waitress looks up from her studies and hesitantly asks the Colonel what he would like. Before he has a chance to answer, a young man in his early twenties hurries over yelling, "No, get out! We don't want you hanging around in here."

Looking the punk straight in the eyes and stopping him in his tracks, I ask, "You talking to me, kid?"

"No sir, I'm speaking to that person!" he says, pointing at the Colonel.

With enough volume to cover the shop and spread out into the lobby, I bring pressure to bear on this little thumb sucker. "The Colonel is with me you little shit and a veteran before you were a twinkle in your daddy's eye. We'll take a seat over by the window while we wait for you to bring our coffee," I smile as he backs away. "If you're not there in five minutes, I'll be on the phone with the VA and then with the news media to see how many cameras we can get here. Next, I'll inform folks right in front of this hotel how you treat vets in this coffee shop. Then, just for kicks and giggles, I'll call the local NAACP and scream that you're a racist." I finish my verbal assault as he heads to the security of the kitchen behind the counter.

Looking around I notice that the Colonel is the only black person in the coffee shop, or for that matter in the hotel lobby. "Is he calling the police? I've been through that before," the Colonel backs away.

"No. By now he's being told by the hotel manager to bring us our coffee and get us out of here as quickly and quietly as he can," I reassure the Colonel.

Within seconds, the young woman from behind the counter appears at our table with two cups of creamed coffee and tells us, "The coffee is on the house."

As she turns to walk away, I call her back and hand her a five dollar bill. After thanking her for the coffee, I quietly tell her to inform the 'twerp' hiding behind the counter that if he comes out here being holier than thou again before we decide to leave, 'I'll be forced to part his ass like the red sea and my foot will be playing the part of Moses'. She smiles nervously and turns back to her counter.

****

While we enjoy our coffee and the nervous discomfort of those around us, the flight from Washington enters it's approach to the Louisville International Airport.

A flight attendant leans down to inform Martin they'll be landing in about twenty minutes and an FBI agent will be waiting for him in the security office.

"If you'll give me your claim check, I'll see that your bag is taken there."

Secret Service Agent Joseph Martin hands her his check, makes another note on his legal pad and then puts it back in the carry-on sitting in the empty seat next to him.

Returning the seat to its upright position, he tightens his seat belt and waits for touchdown.

The Hero

The sun bursting through the window of the coffee shop warms the table as the Colonel tells me that his name is Roger Nichols, that he was a sergeant not a colonel and that he served in the army in Vietnam. With an agonized look, he admits that when he returned home, he had nightmares and turned to alcohol to make them go away.

As we finish our coffee, I realize I still have many more questions to ask my new-found friend and besides; I owe this damaged soul a decent lunch and a drink.

"Let's walk down to the McDonald's at Second and Broadway," I suggest, pushing away from the table.

"Can we go to the Mickey D's at Preston and Market instead?"

"You ashamed to be seen with me?"

"No, I was barred from the one on Broadway."

"I'm shocked." Chuckling, I turn and we head north towards Market Street. "Can I ask about your past and what got you to here? If you don't want to answer because it brings up old memories, I'll understand."

"You want to know how a sixty-year-old-man from a good family can end up walking the streets, stumbling from drink to drink," the Colonel states flatly, looking away.

"That would just about cover it. I need to be assured that I'm not going to end up the same way. When I came home from the war, I was scared of being alone in the dark and of going to sleep. I had nightmares, too. I just need to know it won't happen to me."

Looking down at the sidewalk with tearful eyes, the Colonel confides, "I had the bad dreams too. But, you're going to be alright."

"So far, so good," I smile.

We walk about a block with neither of us having anything to say, as memories of coming home from war click into place, one by one.

****

The plane lands at the Louisville Airport and Agent Martin is escorted off, while the other passengers are still gathering their belongings and moving into the aisle. He walks to the security office to meet his official driver.

After shaking hands, the young FBI agent introduces himself, "I'm Wesley Stone and I'll be your driver while you're here. Headquarters is located downtown Louisville in the Romano L. Mazzoli Building. Would you like to check into your hotel first?"

"Too much to do. I'll check in the hotel later."

The following fifteen minute drive to FBI Headquarters consisted of fragmented 'I know something you don't know' and 'I don't trust you' sentences.

****

Turning onto Market Street en route to the Mickey D's on Preston, the Colonel finally glances up.

"What do you want to be in life?"

"What?"

"Well, I set my goal to reach a level of poverty and I've recently achieved my goal. Is that your goal in life?"

11

"No, that's not what I want out of life and I doubt that's what you want either."

"Well, let me tell you something smart ass. Drinking is a very demanding profession and at my age I can't hold down two jobs," the Colonel settles back into his story and begins again. "I remember that I'd been marking off the days until it was time to come back home on my short-timer calendar. I'd been looking forward to that day for months, seeing my family and friends."

"Yeah, me too," I begin to piece together that time in my life.

"Getting off the plane in the U.S., my smile soon disappeared and I just wanted to get back on the plane. The signs being held up sure weren't welcoming any of us soldiers home. People were spitting on our uniforms, pointing at us and yelling 'baby killer'."

"I know what you're saying, when I got home things weren't any better."

****

After ordering our food at the counter, the judgemental stares of the people standing in line follow us as folks sitting at nearby tables just look hopeful that we were getting our food to go. We stop at a table near the center, just behind the serving bar, and settle in for awhile.

With a mouth full of cheeseburger, the Colonel thanks me and continues his trip down nightmare lane from the war to the bottle. "I found myself a job in a warehouse and signed up for some college classes, but my nights were spent drinking alone." Stopping only long enough to take in a handful of fries he continues, "I started missing work, got fired, dropped out of school and only left my room in the basement to get something more to drink. After a couple months of that, my dad said to get a job or get out.

Taking a drink though the straw in his coke without raising it from the table, he stares for a moment at the top of the cup, trying to hide the tears in his eyes. Finally, glancing up he adds, "I worked odd jobs, kept drinking, and learned to live on the streets."

"What about family?"

"I got hurt real bad once about two years back and EMS took me to the VA. My sister was listed as my next of kin and when it looked like I might die, the hospital called her. Her husband came to get me and they fixed up a room for me. A month later when the meds ran out, the nightmares began again and the alcohol helped."

By now, the people sitting near us had quietly drifted away and the crew started the cleaning up part of the shift. The only evidence we ate at all were the paper bags on the table.

The Colonel stood to go refill his coke.

With many questions still running though my mind, I glance toward the service bar and notice the frightened expression on the face of the young high school girl behind the counter. She was staring at a man with his back to us and his right hand deep in his jacket pocket.

Eight of the ten voices in my head told me to call the police, but hell, when did I ever listen to them? My imaginary friend, the one that runs with scissors, tells me to pick up my coffee, go to the counter and stick my nose in this. So, I stand and head towards the trouble.

Reaching the counter, I ask the girl for more coffee in an attempt to move her away from the man.

"Wait your turn," the young man growls, right hand still deep in his pocket.

"I just want coffee. Are you my waiter?"

"You better mind your own business, old man."

"Just need my coffee refilled, I don't even need cream."

The girl nervously takes my cup, and heads in the direction of the coffeepot.

Pointing at me with his hand still in his pocket, the young puke snarls that if I don't take my old ass back to my seat and sit down, he'll shoot me.

Out of the corner of my eye, I notice the Colonel moving behind the mouthy brat, and without a sound a tray strikes the back of the boy's shoulders putting him on his knees. As both of his empty hands rush forward to break his fall, he's struck again before he can recover.

Stepping on the back of his neck, I keep him from getting to his feet as I check his empty pockets.

Glancing up, I see the Colonel standing there holding a broken tray with a bemused look on his face. "Old man, my ass."

The young lady behind the counter starts yelling about a robbery, while the manager calls the police and everyone begins to gather around the Colonel, thanking him for his heroics and shaking his hand.

Within minutes the police are there, closely followed by a news van.

I'm left staring as this old man who lives without money, house or property and who uses only his wit to survive, gives me insight into my own life. This unmade bed with ears dressed in a dingy green-striped dress shirt, worn brown suit pants, dirty tennis shoes with no laces and a powder blue tie with a hand-printed pink hula girl as a belt is my new life coach.

As the police and the news people interview the Colonel, the other customers and the Mickey D staff recount how the old man took down the robber.

I walk home, feeling good about being friends with a real hero.

Lawyers And Accountants, Or College Kids With Guns

The squad room on the sixth floor of FBI headquarters covers almost the entire floor and is crammed with desks, paired up and pushed together facing one another. The walls are covered with maps and charts, unlike the ones hanging in the hall with poster size pictures of FBI agents taking down would-be bad guys. The hospital green 'fifty by fifty' room, with a white ceiling and brown tile floor, is crowded with college kids armed with badges and handguns. Law and accountant degrees abound and moms and dads all over the country are happy that their college money is being put to good use as their sons and daughters play police. Distrust in the room can be chewed. A group of FBI agents scrutinize the ATF agents as they monitor the DEA agents who are keeping a close eye on the ICE agents, and the whole bunch is worried about who will get the next available money from Washington for new toys.

Martin is seated on the corner of the desk nearest the door, causing the various groups to turn to look at him while he informs the Louisville agents what will be needed from them and the local police department. A meeting has been set for the next morning with the mayor and his staff, as well as staff from the works and police departments. After the meeting, he'll need to meet with the heads of the different locations that will be visited by the First Lady.

"I'll need a list of agents who will be on the detail the whole time, along with the ones who will just be there the day of the detail. But now, I'm going to head over and check in my hotel and try to get some rest. I'll see everybody early tomorrow morning, we have a lot of work to do."

****

Checking my watch as I open the door to our condo, I can't wait for Maureen to get home so I can tell her about the Colonel and the morning we had. I hope he'll have time for coffee tomorrow as I still have questions rolling around in my head. After supper and a movie on the television, it's bedtime.

Sleep comes hard as the questions for tomorrow rush though my head; "When were you in Vietnam? Who were you with? Were you shot? Did you drink before you went?"

Sometime after midnight, I fall asleep.

****

At first light I'm up, dressed and on my way down the stairs to the kitchen. I make coffee, do the clean-up and throw a load of clothes in the washer. So far, I'm maybe three hours ahead of my daily time table and running out of things to do.

Turning on the news, I see that the report of the Colonel's bravery is still being played this morning. Three cups of coffee don't curb my impatience for the gym to open, but if I get there too soon the yuppies will still be there in their matching workout clothes discussing the stock market or possibly the latest tennis or soccer games. To kill time I fix eggs, bacon and toast for breakfast and have them on the table by the time Maureen is downstairs, dressed for the office.

"Breakfast is ready, Sweetie."

"Thanks, but I'm running late for work. See you tonight."

With her out the door, I eat the eggs and bacon and finish cleaning the kitchen. The 'children' should be on their way to their offices by now. The old farts will be on the treadmills decked out in their half-calf white socks with colored stripes around the top, pocket tee shirts and walking shorts, all the while talking sports and watching the young girls.

Fifteen minutes later, I enter the Y's main workout room and tell yesterday's warriors about the Colonel and the kid at the coffee shop. They all agree that they would protest outside the hotel if they don't treat the old guy right. Smiling to myself, I realize that we call the Colonel the 'old guy', when most of us are his age or older. The sixty-year-old flower children, still fighting their part of the war, are saying that the coffee shop has the right to keep that dirty man out of the store and that he has no special rights just because he fought in the military. I leave both sides of the battle reliving the sixties and head for Second and Jefferson looking for the Colonel.

****

I find him sitting on a flowerpot at the Second Street end of the block, in front of the loading dock of the Convention Center and across the street from the hotel. The newly built center covers two city blocks. Ten years back we would be in the middle of a parking lot flanked by the Savoy Theater, the other dirty movie place and the favorite of the high school boys because of the lack of checking ID cards. Gorgotto's Liquor Store was on the far side, which carried mostly fifths of two dollar bottles of wine and half pints of whiskey, the choice of the walk-in trade.

"You remember Gorgotto's?" I ask.

"I shared many a bottle of wine in the back corner of the parking lot behind it. There was a barrel that would get set on fire on winter nights. None of us had guns, but I saw more than one killing at that fire barrel, most with a club or a knife."

"What were the killings about?"

"A lot of things, but mostly because someone took too big of a drink when it was their turn."

"Doesn't seem like something to kill over."

"You're not a drunk. Money gets harder to come by in the winter and everybody is in a hurry to get in out of the cold. The people coming out of their offices or going into work are doing it in the dark when the days are shorter. Women are usually easier to get money out of, they feel sorry for you but in the dark they just want to get to their office or car and get away."

"Let's go get a cup of coffee."

"Where?"

"Same place as yesterday."

"You know they'll call the police this time," the Colonel reminds me that we were not exactly welcomed with open arms.

"You think the police will buy the coffee?"

"We're going to jail."

"The jail got coffee?"

"You're nuts."

"You going?"

"Sure, I'm going. Wouldn't miss it."

Entering the front door of the hotel, I notice a police car parked on the street near the coffee shop door. The Colonel gets that 'I told you so' look on his face and seems sure they're there for us.

"Told you they'd be waiting."

"They're here for coffee. How would they know we were coming?"

I walk up to the counter and tell the college girl we want two cups of coffee, cream only. Out of the corner of my eye I can see the 'thumb sucker' go to the front table and point at us, as he asks the police to make us leave. Glancing over at one of the officers I know, I place my index finger to my lips and turn back toward the counter. The Colonel wants to get the coffee to go, but I'm thinking it's time this kid learns to stop sucking eggs. After asking the Colonel to go get us a seat, I stroll over to the table with the two young officers and the kid.

"Pardon me, could I get you to hold a table for ten in the morning? I'll be having several of my friends meet me here for coffee."

"You can't bring ten street people in here, you hear what I'm saying!" the kid explodes, turning red from head to foot.

"Yeah, I hear you. I'll see you in the morning."

The two officers laugh, but the kid doesn't get the joke.

The Colonel and I pick up our coffee and go sit on a large concrete flower pot in front of the hotel. This doesn't do much for the hotel manager's disposition, as guests coming and going have to pass right by us.

"Do you enjoy being a pain in the ass to these people?"

"Can you get clean clothes for tomorrow?"

"Why?"

"We can have breakfast at Days Inn at their breakfast bar."

"You're nuts. They'll call the police if we do that."

"The daywork people will be on duty and won't know if we're guests or not and won't ask. I think I'd like bacon and waffles for breakfast. What about you?"

We watch as a black sedan passes by real slow, letting the passenger get in and out taking pictures. The Colonel remarks it had already been up and down the street a half a dozen time before I got here.

"Well, if he's looking for Aggie, she hasn't worked this street for ten years or more."

"Who's Aggie?"

"Aggie was a German woman who worked as a hooker on Jefferson Street for years. She worked for a well-to-do couple in the east end as a housekeeper and nanny. They'd bail her out of jail when she got locked up and get her a lawyer. Do you remember much about Jefferson Street?"

Aggie's Boyfriend

"No, I was raised up across the river. I didn't come to Louisville until I went in the service. They had us report in to the drill sergeant at the Greyhound Bus Station on the corner across from Gorgotto's. The buses would come in and the drill instructor would load us up on the bus and take us to Fort Knox for training."

"Did you ever go in Windel's Bar just past the bail bondman's office and down from the bus station?"

"Nah, I made the trip to Fort Knox when I was eighteen years old and my dad and mom brought me to the station."

Reaching back in my memory I remember out loud," I hear Windels was here before World War II, and lots of the soldiers waiting for buses back to the Fort or catching buses back home waited there. Some guys would come to Windel's just to get off the base because they had no place else to go. One of the soldiers painted a mural on the wall that stayed there until the building was torn down to make room for the hotel."

"It makes me sad to see history gone forever," the Colonel muses with a sad tone in his voice.

"Hey, how about lunch at Rally's? Or have you been barred from there too?"

"Sounds okay. Am I going to have to save you there too? Look, it's Aggie's boyfriend again."

We get up and head in the direction of Rally's.

"From the looks of the car I would say that Aggie's boyfriend is a fed," I watch the guy get in and out, taking pictures and making notes.

"What do you think he's looking for?" The Colonel tilts his head like a dog trying to work a math problem.

"Who knows, who cares? Let's go to lunch, I got more questions."

"My question for you is why do you hang out with me? I'm just a drunk without a home, a family or any money."

"You have answers to the questions I need answers to. Why don't you go to the VA and get some help?"

"You ever ask those people for anything? They treat everyone like second class citizens when you ask them for help. First, you have to stand in line to talk to a face with no expression, who hands you a stack of papers that takes hours to fill out. You never get them right the first time. Once finished, you get to sit in a room and answer a lot of questions, after which you are told to come back in three months when you maybe get to see a doctor. Then, you go back to the waiting room only to be told your appointment has been rescheduled. If you die or kill yourself, it's just one less old soldier they have to deal with. Most of the people you see are not medical, they're government appointees who get jobs there and can't be fired."

"Remind me not to ask that question again," I keep walking.

"Look, Aggies's boyfriend is taking pictures of the Wayside Mission."

"He's not FBI, he's Secret Service." I know what's happening now.

"What the hell is the Secret Service doing at a homeless center? Did they find out one of the junkies or drunks is the heir to the throne?" The Colonel laughs at his own joke.

"No, the First Lady's coming to town. She's coming to show the country what a great job the government is doing to help the homeless." The news story comes rushing back in my head.

"Oh, the government has taken care of the homeless and down-trodden all right! They sign them up to vote and use the address of some shelter like the Jefferson Street Baptist Church. On election day they come by in a van and pick up people to drive them to the polls. After you vote, they take you back to where they picked you up and then give you a half pint. They also tell you who you need to vote for by the way, and if you didn't get signed up, they have a list of names you can use to get your half pint."

"I was thinking it was against the law to drink when the polls are open," I remark, knowing that the bars and liquor stores have to close on election day.

"Sure, the bootleg lobby pushed to pass a law so that when the polls are open, or on Sundays, a two-dollar bottle of whiskey costs five dollars. But the van driver gives you a bottle for voting and that's not against the law."

****

Rally's is a great place for us to eat. It's a walk up window and has tables outside so nobody's there to raise hell about the homeless. We have the same for lunch as yesterday; cheeseburgers and fries, but today we add a chocolate milkshake.

"Is there any part of the government you do like?" I turn to the Colonel.

"It's not just the government. It's the shelter people, the courts, the liquor stores and the businesses around where we hang out. The government sends us a check to the mission or to the church. The banks won't cash them because we don't have an account, so we have to go to the liquor store that charges us ten percent to cash our checks, but only if we buy something. You can guess what we buy. Now if we get out of the store with any money, every punk in the neighborhood knows the checks came in and they're waiting to rob us. Then the mission charges us two dollars for a bed and anywhere from fifty cents to a dollar for meals. If you run out of money, you go beg on the street. Oh yeah, everyone is out to help. Help themselves."

Days Inn, Here We Come

This morning I'm changing routine; shower, dress pants, polo shirt and tennis shoes. I'm now ready to meet the Colonel at nine for breakfast at the hotel. No time to fix coffee, but I'll pick one up at McDonald's on the way to First and Liberty. Thursday is a good time to grab a meal at the Inn because it's busy. The guests there on business will be preparing to leave for the week and the next wave of the company crowd will have advance people checking in, along with other folks just in town for the weekend.

With coffee in hand, I find myself once again waiting on the corner for the Colonel. I'm about five minutes early, but he's right on time. He appears from behind the Shell Station dressed in ugly brown sandals, blue jeans and a long sleeve white shirt with the tail out.

"You look like you got stuck in the sixties."

"Hey, it's the best I could do at the Salvation Army Shelter down on Brook Street. Got a bed, a locker, a kit to shave and bath soap."

"You must have had a busy night."

"I had to sit through some Holy Roller pastor for an hour before I could eat supper. It's almost enough to make a man drink. After dinner, I showered and played chess with a one-eyed black guy missing a leg, maybe eighty years old and a left-over from the Korean War. He beat me like a rented mule."

We enter the hotel from the locked poolside door as a lady with both arms full of bags uses her back to push it open. Ambling on down the hall, we pass the sleepy morning faces of people pulling bags, herding kids and double checking to make sure they didn't close their room door with the key still lying on the dresser.

****

Just past the ever present housekeeping cart, we locate the remaining guests in the breakfast bar. The crowded few tables are only free for a minute before being re-occupied, and some guests are asking to share tables with others who have an open chair. We find two chairs at a table near the end of the serving line, closest to the steaming coffee pot. The Colonel gets his plate and dips up eggs, bacon and biscuits covered in gravy. Not one thing he has to wait on.

Not me. I put in a couple of waffles and stand calmly, waiting for the timer to go off.

The Colonel has finished eating and is ready to leave by the time I put my plate on the table and return to the coffeepot for a fill up. The young couple sitting with him had just finished saying, "Have a good day," as I'm taking a chair.

I watch as the Colonel stops chewing his bite of egg and moves to the edge of the chair, obviously preparing himself to break for the door.

"What the hell's wrong with you?"

"It's Aggie's boyfriend."

"It sure is. If he comes over for coffee, we can ask if he'd like to sit with us."

"You're crazy you know. He's some kind of agent and we're stealing breakfast."

"There are no other chairs, and he's not the hotel dick." I'm now having a good time with the Colonel.

Aggie's boyfriend gets his coffee and joins two other men at a table on the other side of the room.

We finish our meal, get a cup of coffee to go and stroll out the front door with toothpicks in the corner of our mouths like we belonged. Noticing Agent Martin sitting at his table talking on his cell phone, I decide the other men had to be agents too or he wouldn't be talking in front of them.

I give the Colonel five dollars to help him though the day and start for home.

As I turn the corner onto Broadway, I see Agent Martin, along with the two men he met at breakfast and the director of the City Works Department, standing in front of Wayside Mission with a street map. Edging closer, I can hear Martin noting certain streets that need to be tagged for no parking on both sides, and then explaining that all mailboxes and garbage cans will need to be removed. The director, maps and notes in hand and feeling his importance to the assignment, is off to his workplace.

As Martin and the other two agents enter the lobby to talk to the head of the mission, I slip in behind them and move to a corner to hide behind a plastic ficus tree, its base filled with discarded cigarette butts.

I watch as Reverend Morris shakes hands with Martin and leads the way to his office, once the manager's office of the old Holiday Inn. The rugs along the hallway are dark and stained and more than one light is burned out or has been stolen for one of the rooms. Most of the office furniture has been to the Goodwill more than once, showing it's history in multiple stains and scars.

Martin, talking more to the two agents than the reverend, tells them that all halls have to be cleaned and all lights are to be working for the First Lady's visit.

"We'll get the works department to send people over tonight."

"Okay, let's get to the dining room and wherever the First Lady will meet with the children."

"This way, gentlemen," Morris points back towards the lobby.

The large dining room housed a mismatch of wobbly card tables and battered metal folding chairs, a few wooden picnic tables riddled with splinters, six round wooden kitchen tables, an assortment of unmatched chairs and what appears to be the remains of a grade-school steam table.

"This'll need some work also and we'll need a place for the press. Make sure there's a clean chair for the First Lady."

"Will the First Lady be eating with us?"

"Hardly. She'll be coming from a luncheon and will barely have enough time to be shown the eating area and meet a few of the people volunteering in the kitchen. Make sure they're from a church, people like it when the church people get involved. Now, will the kids be in here or do you guys have a playroom?" Martin asks, waving his finger in a half-arc taking in the dining hall.

"The playroom is just up those stairs in the old ballroom."

Reverend Morris leads Martin and the agents towards the winding stairway to the right of the lobby.

"I have to meet the fundraiser people, but you two know what the First Lady wants for her press shots. We're going to need three children; one boy and two girls, age's six to eight. Make sure they're clean and have the boy missing a front tooth. I want to meet all these people tonight, the First Lady will be in town first thing tomorrow morning," Martin continues to shout orders as he walks away, leaving the reverend and the two agents standing there.

It Takes The Government
To Make The Homeless, Homeless

Back at the condo, I fix a glass of sweet tea and ready myself for a little television and maybe a nap. But, what I see out my kitchen window shocks even me. There's a homeless man, about fifty, pissing on my garage door.

Sprinting down the stairs, I burst out the front door yelling, "What the hell do you think you're doing?"

"Had to go," says the man turning from the wall to face me with his clothes in disarray, no sign of embarrassment that his dick was still in his hand.

"You could go to some place like McDonald's there on the corner and use the restroom."

"The people from the mission are all up there. The government threw them out."

"What do you mean the government threw them out?"

"The FBI came in and told us we had to get out cause the First Lady is coming. They say she's coming to visit us and find out what we need."

"Well, you can't piss back here."

Between the buildings, I can see McDonald's parking lot and the sidewalk across the street from Wayside crowded with the mission people. As I move to the corner, I discover the police outside trying to get the homeless cleared off Mickey D's parking lot to make room for the lunch customers.

Inside, the police are forcing the squatters from inside the restaurant back out into the parking lot, replacing the group now moving down the street to the sidewalk in front of the college across from the mission. This moved the people on the sidewalk to the college parking lot between the parked cars and caused the people from between the cars to move over to the parking lot of the McDonald's. And around and around they go. This is better than television.

Taking a seat on the wall in front of the college parking lot, I watch and listen to the street people. It's their world, a place I'm no longer a part of and no longer know the participants personally. The people I look on from afar are just like any other community. They have their good and bad members. They've banded together today against the government and the First Lady because they put them out of what they consider their home, as if they have the right to push them around willy-nilly. Where's the Colonel when I need him to translate what's happening? One lady in baggy jeans and a tee shirt is holding a baby on her hip swaying back and forth, while another tall skinny lady standing on the curb between the sidewalk and the driving area yells at the building itself, as if it had done something wrong. Most are talking in groups with lots of frowns and hand gestures. I don't have to hear the words to know these are some unhappy people and the First Lady is not high on their popularity poll. A group of men and women, standing near one of the light standards just to my right, are asking why there are children still in the playroom, but their kids were put out on the street.

I spot the works department truck heading up Broadway picking up the garage cans, as another truck with a work crew, followed by a police car with its lights on, is welding the manhole covers in place. As the group sees the postal truck begin removing the mail boxes a wave of gossip gets started with, 'The post office is going to stop picking up the mail', and 'The First Lady is coming to tell them that Kentucky is no longer a part of the United States'. A lady leaning against a nearby light standard asks how they would get their checks now and from whom. A nearby group picked up on this worry, with one man saying he heard one of the agents talking about cutting off checks. He had firsthand knowledge and people gather to learn what he knew. Another said he had heard something about the checks on the radio. The lady with the baby is asking anyone that would listen, "What am I going to do if they cut off my checks?"

"We'll riot, that's what we'll do," yells another woman.

"Let's do it while the First Lady is here, so the press will see and we'll be all over the news."

"We'll have to get the word to the other shelters because they'll lose their checks too. They need to meet us here tomorrow to help."

****

The agents working inside the mission find the lightbulbs are working, cleaning is underway, carpets have been cleaned and there's even a new-looking chair for the First Lady, wrapped in paper so as to not get dirty. A female agent is talking to a group of children over in a corner, choosing the three children who will meet the First Lady.

The boys, standing all in a row, are being asked questions to see how they'll answer. If they're too shy or too smart, they just won't do. The agent asks them all to smile and finds one with a big gap where two upper front teeth once lived. He has on dark blue shorts pinned on the side with a safety pin so they'll fit, high top tennis shoes with no socks and a tee shirt that hung off his shoulders and tucked in his shorts, preventing it from covering his knees. His hair is homecut, short but neat, and he's very well spoken for a young fella of eight.

The girls are lined up the same way and two six-year-olds are chosen. Their mothers have dressed them in hand-me-down dresses about a size too big, but clean. The taller of the two has short brown hair trimmed with scissors straight around just off the shoulder, and big brown eyes staring out from under bangs cut at an angle. The other young lady has red curls that bounce when she shakes her head, bright blue eyes and a mischievous smile that lights up her freckled face.

The agent tells the children's mothers to make sure they're clean in the morning and maybe not dressed in their best clothes. One of the male agents enters the room pushing a young boy in a wheel chair, smiling at what he's found. The female agent exclaims, "Great job," as if the agent has put him in the chair personally.

The Other End Of The Money Rule

Two cars carrying Martin and three FBI agents drive slowly along the half-circled driveway to the front of the Brown's estate. Six wide steps lead up to a double oak door framed by frosted glass windows, reminding them of a castle. The door is the center point of a two-story red brick house that covers nearly a whole city block. It's surrounded with six-foot boxwood hedges, protecting the small, but well-groomed, yard from the view of the street. Surveying the immediate area from the top of the steps, Martin rings the doorbell and is surprised when Mr. Brown himself opens the door and invites them inside.

Ed Brown appears out of place, dressed in jeans and a faded polo shirt while the agents are in coats and ties. Standing in a foyer housing a fountain located directly under an enormous skylight, Martin introduces the agents assigned to work with him and his staff for the luncheon.

Mr. Brown directs them to call him Ed, but Martin informs him that they can't do that. It's against policy. Turning to look Martin in the eye, Ed barks, "I'm giving a fifty-thousand dollar a plate lunch for the President of the United States. If you won't address me as Ed, with one phone call I can get someone in here who'll call me Humpty Dumpty if I tell him to."

"Then, Ed it will be."

"Good. Now the front circle will be kept clear for the First Lady and a cover will be in place for her exit from the limo and up to the door. Guests will already be inside before she arrives. All other cars will be moved to the lot across the street by valets and we'll have EMS standing by in the rear. A list of my staff has been sent to the White House for clearance. Your team is to be fed on the patio, along with staff and news reporters, before the First Lady arrives. Once she's here, no one will be allowed to enter. Is there anything else I need to do?" Glancing over at Martin, he waits for a response.

"No, sir. I'll see to everything else. We'll have to have access to your home around eight tomorrow morning."

"That'll be fine. We'll be up, but may need our bedroom and bath to be closed a bit longer as it'll take the wife awhile to get ready you know. I'm going to leave you to get your work done, but if you need me I'll be around."

"Yes sir, thank you."

As Ed walks to the back of the house to grab a sandwich from the cooks in the kitchen, Martin begins handing out the assignments. "Patterson, I want you to take the outside. You'll have six agents and ten local officers. Half of the officers will be in plain clothes and are trained for this kind of security. The other half will be in uniform and can be used for traffic and crowd control if necessary. Conely, you've got the inside including the front door. You'll have ten troops, half are ours and half local, plain clothes and all trained. O'Malley, you handle the staff and any neighborhood complaints. And there will be some. We'll give you two uniforms, just in case they aren't fans of the President. Do your best to not lock anyone up. That means your biggest job is to keep the locals under control. They don't like or trust you and they sure don't like rich people who think they are above the law. It'll only take one, 'Do you know who my daddy is' from some entitled little brat, to get the whole block locked up. They have the power, but you have the wits to stop them."

****

Still sitting on the wall across from the mission, I watch the crowd get larger and louder. This really was better than television. The Colonel walks up from behind me and sits down.

"What's going on?" I ask, turning to read his expression.

"I think they're mad."

"No shit. I got that part, but why?"

"The word down at the shelter is that they're gonna riot tomorrow because the government is stopping their checks. They're making signs and getting the word out in all directions," he briefs me with insight gained in the last hour, having had coffee with a few angry folks wandering in and out of the nearby shelter.

"Yeah, I've been sitting here listening. Seems this got started because they put them out on the street while they get ready for the First Lady's visit."

"There's an old bag lady down on Brook Street telling everybody that she's gonna kill the bitch. Of course, she's always gonna kill somebody. Too many drugs, I guess."

"Anything to worry about?"

"A drunk old broad looking to kill somebody is always something to be worried about."

"You got a name?"

"Nope. Just an angry old white woman about fifty, but looks to be about ninety. Why?"

"I know one or two police who'll be around tomorrow. I'll get the word to them."

"Hell, I know one or two police myself, but I don't tell 'em shit," spits the Colonel, walking away.

"See you tomorrow for coffee?"

"Sure. Where?"

"The Five Star Service Station over on the corner. I'll buy."

"Gonna piss anybody off?"

"I'll do my best."

"That's what I'm afraid of."

"Nine o'clock?"

"I'll be there," the Colonel shouts over his shoulder.

The Big Day

Martin is up before four; showered, shaved and dressed in his uniform black suit, tailored to fit over his gun and radio along with any other equipment necessary for a detail. Today the First Lady would arrive and he'd be in that same suit and tie all day, with no time from 'touchdown' to 'wheels up' to change again. Martin wolfs down a bagel he'd picked up the night before at a service station on the corner and a cup of 'made in the room' hotel coffee. No eating in your detail suit.

First order of the day, meet the plane from DC carrying the vehicles for the detail and scheduled to land around six. The plane will be routed to a large hanger near the Air National Guard area to offload the three black SUVs and one black limo. Martin's plan is to be there to oversee the unloading as part of his duties, although mainly leaving the work on the vehicles to the crew that travels with the cars; washing, waxing, fueling and spot-cleaning on the inside. Bottled water will be placed in the refrigerator and the secure phone in the back seat of the limo would be tested. Nothing will be overlooked. Everything must be just right; not only for the First Lady but also for Agent Polly Harris who will accompany her.

Harris is a six-foot tall former college basketball star with the best-looking legs Martin had ever seen. She's also the personal agent to the First Lady and the love of Martin's life. Just thinking about those long tan legs in skimpy running shorts sprinting down the track made his heart race. Dating of agents on the detail was frowned on by the Secret Service and if the bosses found out about their romance, one of them might be removed from the detail, so secrecy was paramount. But right now, Martin has to make sure everything is ready for the First Lady. Polly will have to wait.

The team of agents assigned to be in the vehicles are scheduled to be at the hanger by seven to check their onboard weapons and guard the cars until they pick up the First Lady, her two personal secretaries and Agent Harris. Martin watches from the corner of the hanger, making a point to keep his suit clean and out of harm's way as everything is unloaded.

The mechanics had just begun washing the limo when a Learjet comes to a stop near the front of the hanger. Martin walks to the tip of the wing as the plane's door opens and nine agents disembark in their travel clothes; jeans, dark blue Secret Service polo shirts, aviator sunglasses and each carrying black suit bags slung over their shoulder. In turn, they all shake hands with Martin, sit their bags over to the side and get to work setting up the cars as the mechanics finish up.

Martin meets with the team leader, going over the plans for the day. "The second agents will cover the entry as the First Lady arrives and the drivers will stay with the cars. There'll be two marked police cars from the local department to lead you to the house. These officers will stay with the cars and drivers and they're yours to use as you see fit. There will also be local cops at the intersections to block traffic. There'll be food on the back patio for your guys, but only one or two at a time. As always, the detail comes first. Any questions? Good, then I'll see you at the house."

****

In the meantime, I find the Colonel standing on the corner near the gas station holding a paper bag, dressed in another pair of jeans and a blue dress shirt with the tail out. His hair is combed and his tennis shoes are tied.

"Living down on Brook Street is starting to show on you."

"Yeah, I'm a real gentleman. I got sandwiches to eat with our coffee."

"From the mission?"

"No, Mickey D's."

"You didn't have to buy me breakfast. I know your money's tight."

"Here, have an Egg McMuffin and stop worrying about my money."

Unwrapping a muffin and taking a bite, I hand him a cup of coffee."Don't buy me food any more, save your money. I'm trying to get you off the street."

"You could take me home with you," laughs the Colonel.

"You know what I mean. Let me give you your money back on these sandwiches. How much did you spend?"

"Nothing, they were free."

"Did you steal them?"

"You mean like you did yesterday at the hotel? I got them out of the dumpster. They throw 'em out at the end of the breakfast meal.

"The dumpster? Really? Wish you'd told me that before I started on my second one."

"They were all wrapped. Stop being a girl about it."

"What's the word about the First Lady's visit to the mission?" I ask, looking for info that might help keep her safe.

"Everybody is talking about being here and the crazy old bag lady is still talking about shooting the bitch. I have to guess she's talking about the First Lady. The group from Brook Street is talking about coming here with signs and blocking the street, demanding to speak with her. The word is out that the government is cutting off welfare and food stamps."

"You coming up?"

"Sure, I'll be there."

"If you see that woman tell one of the agents, okay?"

"You bet. You're coming?" asks the Colonel

"Maybe."

****

Martin gets a feel as to how his day will go before he can pull his car in front of the Brown estate. A uniform officer directs him to move to the lot across the street. He shows his credentials to the officer who silently points to the area across the street where the rest of the Secret Service cars are already parked.

"I'll just be here for a few minutes."

"Yeah, I'm sure. Across the street, buddy."

Before Martin can escalate this to the next level, Agent Patterson appears at the car door. Martin feels that the tide is turning his way, but Patterson climbs in the car and directs Martin to the area across the street.

"Damn, Martin. You've been at this for a long time. These uniform officers don't want to be here. Some are on overtime, but the plain clothes officers are here because they're trained for this job and are assigned to these details."

"I'm the Secret Service and just so happen to be in charge. Who does that little pimp think he is?"

"He doesn't trust you and he sure don't like you. He was following your orders and has the power to pull you out of the car, lock you up, tow your car and become a hero to the rest of the force. Would it be worth it to you to be right and not have to walk about a hundred feet?"

"Okay, you're right. It's been a long day and these guys do a good job. It's the FBI they don't trust."

"We're all from the government and we're supposed to be here to help them," Patterson reminds me, smiling for the first time today.

Check And Recheck

Before Martin and Patterson can walk back across the street, Conely is standing on the front steps.

"You've got to talk to him."

"Well, where is he?"

"In the kitchen having coffee with my team, calling the President Johnny and talking about how they flew in the Air Guard together. Just follow the laughter."

Martin walks into the kitchen at the end of a story as Ed Brown laughs and says, "Alcohol may have been involved."

"Mr. Brown, I mean Ed, may I have a word with you?"

"Sure, agent. Guys, I really enjoyed coffee this morning."

Turning to Martin, he continues, "Now, what can I do for you?"

"The metal detector at the front door. I have to have it."

"You bet. We want the First Lady to feel safe, not just be safe. The cook said that you never know when someone will try something. Anything else?"

Martin walked away shaking his head and activates his radio, telling Conely to put the metal detector up, the cook has okayed it.

"Did you say that Cook okayed it? Who's Cook?" questions Agent Conely

"He's the guy that makes the soup. Just put it up, I have to see the gardener about the placement of the agents."

"What the hell are you talking about?"

"Don't ask, just set up the machine. It's nine thirty, my head hurts and I still need to go to the mission and check the airport team," Martin mutters to himself with the radio keyed.

"Will you be on point for the First Lady?" asks Conely.

"Yes, but you'll take your cues from Agent Harris, she'll be with her. You and Patterson got the lunch detail and I'm on my way to the mission. Wheels down between eleven and eleven thirty."

"We got it, boss."

Martin pulls onto the mission's parking lot that now sports two mission buses painted gray with Wayside hand-painted in bright burgundy on the sides. Numerous marked and unmarked police cars crowd the lot and several agents are standing around waiting. A uniformed officer is standing guard at every door and several others are gathered together looking across the street, all the while listening to their radios.

Once out of his car at the main entrance, Martin walks over to see what's of interest. The entire homeless population of Louisville appears to be standing on the sidewalk. "What's going on?"

One of the uniforms answers, "They've been over there since we put them out of the mission this morning and the group keeps growing."

"Well, get 'em out of here," orders Martin.

"Okay. How?"

"I don't need this now. Tell me what happened?"

Agent Davis, who's running the team at the mission, turns to Martin, "This morning we cleared the building so we could check it for bombs and declare it safe. Once it had been cleared, we couldn't let the residents back in. The people in the kitchen were cleared, and the kids who were chosen to talk to the First Lady were placed in the playroom. They're coming from all over the city because they heard that the government is going to stop their welfare money."

"Are you going to be able to keep them in check?"

"We've asked for more police, just before the First Lady gets here," offers the uniform as Davis and Martin start inside to inspect the set-up.

"The rugs were cleaned the best they could, but some burn holes and wear spots couldn't be covered. Works department got the lights on in the hall but then had to replace several bulbs that were stolen during the night. We had a clean chair brought in from City Hall that doesn't look too out of place and Agent Wharton has the children in the playroom. There are two little white girls about six years old wearing bad fitting hand-me-downs, a black kid who's missing two front teeth that everyone is in love with, and a young Hispanic boy in a wheel chair."

"You guys got things under control then. Keep me updated on the group across the street. I'll head on over to the airport, touchdown is in less than an hour," Martin says, climbing into his car.

****

Pulling into the airport hanger, Martin smiles for the first time today. The maintenance crew is standing inside the door of the hanger and the cars are lined up in a row and shining in the sunlight. The agents, now dressed in their black suits, are waiting nearby to move to the tarmac. No Ed Brown getting security information from the cook, no cops telling him where to park and no crowd of homeless people mad at the First Lady.

The radio interrupts his peaceful moment with, "Tempo is on the ground. Touchdown. Repeat, Tempo is on the ground."

"All stations stand by, touchdown."

"Detail one is standing by."

"Detail two, standing by."

"This is detail leader. See you at detail one."

"Leader, this is detail one. O'Malley, we have a problem here."

"What has Brown done now?"

"Not Brown. One of the young men who lives in the neighborhood. It seems we don't know who his daddy is."

"I'm on the way, try to control it. If not, get 'Officer Friendly' to speak to him."

"I'll do that, but he says he's having a few of his college buddies over for a football game in his front yard. Thinks he's a lawyer, knows his rights."

"Tell him that Mr. Brown is having a luncheon for the First Lady and we need to control the street for security reasons."

"Seems he's not a big fan of Mr. Brown or the First Lady. The officer said he was a left-wing, tree-hugging…, well you get the idea," O'Malley answered.

"Let him in because he lives there, but keep his buddies off the street."

"I think I'll let Officer Friendly handle that."

****

Martin takes his place at the foot of the steps and waits for the limo to come to a stop as the college kid starts yelling. His friends, who had parked someplace else and walked through backyards, arrive and join him shouting about the war and killing civilians. The officers walk over to engage them until the First Lady was safely in the house.

Once the limo stops and the door opens, Martin takes the First Lady's hand and helps her from the car. Ed Brown steps up to greet her just as Martin becomes aware that Agent Harris is standing behind him. He inhales the scent of her perfume and can see her in his mind's eye. She's wearing a fitted black pants suit that makes you wonder where her gun and radio could possibly be hidden out of sight. Her blond hair was up in a bun with a small curly wire running from her ear to her upturned jacket collar. She has her hand to her mouth talking into her palm, advising the airport detail that Tempo is secure at detail one.

The young men across the street are yelling, "NO MORE WAR, NO MORE WAR!", while the uniform officers and the boxwood hedge block off most of the sound and all sight of the group. The First Lady enters the front door without looking back, followed by Agents Martin and Harris who touch fingers, almost by accident. The guests, gathered in the foyer, applaud as they part to allow Ed Brown and the First Lady to enter the dining room. Everyone else follows, taking their assigned places at the tables marked by name tags, placed according to the amount of contribution. The more you give, the closer you get and some will even get a chance to have their picture taken with her.

On To The Mission

After a brief meal and the pictures have all been taken, one of her secretaries tells the First Lady that it's time to leave for the mission. She begins to move toward the front door, and then down the steps to the limo in the shadow of the canvas. The news cameras and reporters are on the far side, flanked by the two black SUVs. All three agent drivers are sitting alert in their seats with motors running. Second agents are standing by the back passenger doors. Harris walks just to the right of the First Lady while Martin waits in his car, ready to go to the mission as soon as the First Lady is, once again, safely in her limo.

Without warning, a young man in shorts and a football jersey runs past Martin's car and up the driveway with something in his right hand. Every eye strains to see what's in the young man's hand, as Harris and two other agents surround the First Lady and move her back into the house and away from the door. The news people, with their focus on the door, aren't aware at first of what's happening behind them.

Martin leaps from his car and is at once knocked down by two uniform officers chasing the boy across the lawn. About twenty feet from the limo, the kid raises his hand to eye level, just as a Secret Service agent jumps between him and the First Lady. The uniform officers tackle him much like linebackers going after a quarterback.

Back on his feet, Martin is on the kid like ugly on an ape, while fighting his fear that this boy aimed to shoot at his Polly.

The agent who had but seconds before stepped between the boy and the First Lady, holds up a camera yelling, "It's a camera. Only a camera. He just wanted a picture."

One of the officers, having yanked the kid from the ground and is now shoving him into the back of a police car, snaps, "I'll get him a picture. And some fingerprints too. Hold me out at the book."

"O'Malley, you need to get over on that side of the street. The neighbor, who's a lawyer by the way, is on the phone and wants to speak to someone about the boy we just locked up."

"I'm busy with the First Lady. Handle it, or better yet let Officer Friendly talk to him."

"The neighbor kid is going from agent to agent telling them that his father is a lawyer and wants to speak to them."

"Point the kid to Officer Friendly and let him talk with the dad, they'll be handling the case in court. We'll be long gone."

"Okay. Over here kid, I've got somebody to talk to your daddy."

"Just great. Okay, hand it over, kid," Officer Friendly growls into the cell phone, "My name is Officer Hill. Who am I speaking with?"

"I'm David Adams. I'm a lawyer and Tommy's dad."

"I can't see your bar card, but this young man has been telling us you're a lawyer and you're going to have our jobs. So, what can I do for you while I'm still employed?"

"The boy that you gentlemen arrested made a mistake. Could I get you to just maybe give him a ticket and we'll deal with it in court?"

"First, if your son and his friends hadn't done their damnedest to make our job as hard as they could and your kid insisted on telling us that we didn't know who his daddy was, this may have been worked out. Now, looks like your son's friend is gonna have to pay the price for the whole group."

"But the boy just made a mistake, officer. Didn't you make any mistakes when you were a kid?"

"Sir, there are mistakes like wearing white after Labor Day and then there are mistakes like invading Russia in the winter. See you in court." He ends the conversation and hands the phone back to the kid with a 'tired of dealing with your nonsense' look on his face.

The First Lady and Agent Harris begin to move toward the car while Martin tells them about the kid running up in the front yard, and reassures them that everything is under control. Adams must have spoken to his son, because he and all his buddies had all disappeared into the house.

Martin was finally en route to the mission.

****

After my early morning trip to the gym where the topic of the day was the First Lady's visit and I find the hawks and the doves of the sixties at odds on the issue, I'm off to the coffee shop at Second and Jefferson looking for the Colonel. The young man in charge appears relieved that I'm alone, but keeps watching out the window, hoping not to see the Colonel and eight more of his friends. I have my cup of coffee and begin to watch for the Colonel myself, adding to the young man's worries.

Not seeing the Colonel anywhere near on the street, I start for the condo deciding how to spend my day now that I don't have the Colonel to talk with and tell stories. The answer comes as I get closer to Broadway. The crowd on the sidewalk is growing by the minute; news vans and cameras in the mission's parking lot, homeless folks with signs standing in groups, people milling around who only want to see the First Lady and scores of college kids who are just being nosey.

After wading though the sea of humanity to get a can of coke at the gas station, I work my way to the brick wall that divides the McDonald's parking lot from the sidewalk. Not wanting to be too close, I find a seat. To my left is a pair of hardcore members of the local quality control team of cheap wine, well into their self-appointed duties. On my right are two college kids maybe eighteen years old, sucking down burgers and fries and washing them down with large drinks. They don't have a clue about what's going on, but it's better than sitting in class.

Finishing my drink, I spot a woman digging aluminum cans out of the garbage and I throw my empty one in her shopping cart. She looks at me with bloodshot eyes and informs me that she'll kill me. I think I've found the Colonel's bag lady.

Barricades have been placed on the sidewalk across from the mission in the hope that the crowd will stay behind them and traffic has now been blocked for the First Lady's caravan. I spot the Colonel midway down the block in front of a group of folks with 'We need our checks' and 'How will we live' signs.

I watch as the caravan turns into the parking lot where Aggie's boyfriend is waiting to open the door and help the First Lady out of the car, as it pulls to a stop under the front entrance carport. Reverend Morris, dressed in a wool shirt and bib overalls, greets her enthusiastically. The crowd is yelling, "Leave our money alone!" and even the two winos and the college kids without a clue are yelling right along.

As the First Lady, her female agent and Aggie's boyfriend disappear into the mission, I scan the crowd to find the bag lady, who's now wandering down the other side of the street in front of the college.

With the First Lady out of sight, there's nothing for the people to do but yell at the building. And drink. They keep going in and out of the McDonald's and the service station across the street to use the restrooms. They had been going into the college buildings, but now the doors were locked and they had to show a school ID to get in. Given the large number of people, combined with the drinking and the shortage of restrooms, people start peeing between the cars, at the back of McDonald's or just right on the light poles. Two colleges kids are about to have sex on the wall, so I give up my seat to move to the 'walk, don't walk' sign on the corner to give them their privacy.

Meeting The Kids

The First Lady, accompanied by the Reverend, a half dozen Secret Service agents and around that many local police, steps just inside the door and glances around the lobby. With a puzzled look on her face, she was led into the dining room by Agents Harris and Davis. Stopping inside the doorway and seeing only servers from the church, she asks Harris in a low whisper, "Where is everyone?"

"They're all outside, ma'am. They were put outside when they cleared the building."

"Well, no wonder they're mad. If you came to my house and put me in the street because someone was coming to visit, I'd be mad too."

"But ma'am, it's for your safety."

"This is a shelter for women, children and families, agent. Get them in here and feed them."

"But..."

"No buts! Get them in here now and find me an apron. I'm going to help serve."

****

I see the Colonel across the street talking to other street people and pointing at something near the McDonalds. I recognize the two men talking to the Colonel from before in the McDonald's. The fact that they're waving their arms and looking intense doesn't tell me much. I've learned that waving arms and everyone talking at the same time is the way of the street. They could be talking about the location of the nearest restroom, or even a bomb. The thing that worries me is that they're pointing in the direction of the bag lady.

I'd like to get to the Colonel to find out what's happening, but the street is blocked and no one can cross. A few of the mission staff is moving through the group telling the residents they're being checked in at the pool door for dinner. The women and children begin moving toward the mission, but the crowd is only cut by a small number. Seems most of the group consists of people from other homeless missions and college kids hanging out between classes.

****

The First Lady is standing behind the steam table serving mashed potatoes and speaking to each person as they come through the line. Finally, taking off her apron, she walks around to all the tables, listens patiently to their stories and has the White House photographer take a picture with anyone wanting a momento.

Martin announces to the kids in the room that the First Lady will soon start story time in the playroom and she and Agent Davis lead a parade of children and parents up the stairs. The First Lady takes a seat in the chair earmarked for her, letting the kids gather round sitting on the floor. She smiles as she finds herself surrounded by innocent eyed children smiling up at her with peanut butter and jelly smudged faces and squirming little butts, jockeying for position so that their dirty little fingers might get an opportunity to just touch the pretty lady. Smiling, she motions to one of the news reporters standing near and in a low voice says, "This reminds me of when I was a librarian." The news reporter, a young lady trying hard to get a break in the business, smiles and is beside herself that the First Lady spoke to her, just her. She looks at the camera man, asking with her eyes, "Did you get that?" Nodding 'yes', the old camera man smiles, knowing he'll have to make copies for her, her mom and dad, her sisters and brothers, and would bet it gets hung somewhere in the bar where the news people hang out after work.

The handpicked children are seated carefully near the First Lady to ensure they're in the picture. The wheelchair is rolled into place right next to her and the young boy places his hand on the arm of her chair. On her other side are the two little girls and at her feet sits Billy, the kid with the missing front teeth. He's already the media favorite with the whistling sound that's made when he talks, due to his missing teeth. He gives the cameras a wave and a big ole smile.

Agent Harris hands the First Lady a book from the large bag one of the secretaries is carrying. Almost on cue, the room becomes quiet as she holds up a brand new copy, dust jacket still crisp and clean, of *Horton Hears a Who,* written by Dr. Seuss. Pointing at the picture of Horton sitting in the tree she tells them, "This book reminds me of the President."

Billy asks the First Lady if the President climbs trees. Everyone in the room laughs as the First Lady answers, "If I don't watch him every minute."

Opening the book and holding it so all the children can see the pictures, she starts to read, "On the 15th of May, in the jungle of Nool…"

Once the story is finished, the First Lady motions for Billy to come stand beside her. Taking an ink pen from Agent Harris, she signs the inside of the book and then smiling at him, she asks if he would take it to his school library.

"Yes ma'am, I will. And thank you," Billy whistled.

"You are most welcome, young man."

The kids jump to their feet and gather around Billy, wanting to touch the special book. Looking with their fingers, they mark it with their own sticky signatures.

****

Still standing on the corner, I watch the Colonel trying to talk to the agents and officers on the street and getting brushed away like an annoying fly with a wave of their hands. Something tells me they can't be bothered with a street drunk, they're just too busy or maybe just too important to listen to him. I can't get to him from my location, but I look around hoping to see what he sees. These people I've dealt with as an officer my whole career all seem the same. What am I missing?

*****

With the agents and officers ready at the cars, the First Lady refuses to be hurried as the White House photographer takes more pictures with the kids and the parents. She points the news people toward the kids, hoping they'll talk about Horton.

At the request of the Secret Service, the local police stop the children and the group at the top of the steps, enabling the cameras to get some footage of the First Lady on the stairs. The Secret Service is busy trying to get her down the second story stairs safely from the crowd of children that hang on her every word and continue to move closer, just wanting to hug or touch the First Lady.

The crowd outside, still carrying their signs and yelling, have all been pushed back. The limo is parked at the door and the black SUVs and their drivers are ready in place. Marked police cars are on the street with lights on, ready to move the circus and all that came with it out of town. This time tomorrow they'll be back to caring for the people who pay their salaries, or at least tell them they do.

The First Lady is just inside the door, shaking hands with the church servers and mission staff, thanking them for having her. Outside, the Colonel is trying to talk to the agent standing near the parking lot of the mission, but the agent again appears to be too busy. The Colonel yells and points down the street, causing two officers to come up behind him and pull his arms back.

All I can think is, "Well, that's just great, he's getting arrested."

Everything Goes Wrong

As the Colonel is being led to a police car near the intersection across from where I'm standing, he suddenly jerks away and runs at a man that has stepped off the curb and out into the street. At the same time, the First Lady and Agent Harris are being helped into the car by Aggie's boyfriend. I can hear the Colonel yelling, "No! No!", while running full speed at the guy in the street, with the police hot on his heels.

As I watch, the man pulls a gun from under his shirt and points it in the direction of the limo. Time slows to one grain of sand at a time. The first shot has the crowd running in all directions as police hustle into spots behind nearby walls and cars, their guns out and ready. While one six-foot tall police officer tries, with little success, to disappear behind a street sign, the FBI and the Secret Service rush to the limo to protect the First Lady.

Without taking my eye off the scene, I reach to pull my automatic from the holster under my coat, an act that seems to take forever. As the shooter brings his pistol to eye level for his second shot, the Colonel turns in a ballet-like move and falls face first into the pavement. With his hands cuffed behind his back, he has no way of breaking his fall. I see blood on the back of his shirt, spreading out onto the pavement. He isn't moving and I know he's been hit, but how bad?

Most of the crowd is still running or hiding and I realize that the shooter and I are the only ones standing upright. I turn to run and check on the Colonel when the second shot is discharged. Turning my attention from my friend to the sound of the shot, I watch as, trying to fire a third time, he finds his gun jammed. He turns to face me, then looking down at the gun walks right at me.

Martin falls into the side of the car as his left leg gives way from the through-and-through shot to his hip. Agent Polly Harris pulls Martin into the limo, yelling to anyone who will listen to her that he's been shot and the First Lady yells at the driver to get them started for the hospital. Harris, in a panic, looks at the First Lady, and cries that he has to be okay, she loves him.

"Sorry ma'am, I know that we're not supposed to be dating, but it never interfered with our duties. We didn't tell anyone in the service because we both want to keep our jobs at the White House," Polly confesses.

"Bless your heart, dear. That's one of the worst kept secrets in a town where no one can keep their mouths shut. The director met with the President and myself to see if we had a problem with it months ago."

The limo driver yells at a uniform officer standing by that we're going to take Agent Martin to the hospital. The uniform tells him that for gun shots, University Hospital's Room Nine is the best in the state and where all first responders are taken when they're injured.

"Then let's go," the driver yells and puts the vehicle in gear, ready to roll.

The officer alerts the radio they're starting to University ER with the First Lady, and almost simultaneously the radio operator screams into the mike, "The First Lady's been shot?"

As they take off, the driver tells the First Lady and Harris that the police are taking them to University Hospital. He moves out close behind the patrol car with full lights and sirens screaming, as other police cars begin to move into place to stop traffic for the six block ride to the ER. Not knowing the world is about to hear she's been shot, the First Lady assumes her mother role and reassures Harris and Martin that everything will be all right. Over his radio, her driver tells the Secret Service they're on the way to the hospital with Agent Martin. Numerous police cars have now appeared on every corner to block traffic and the Mayor and Chief of Police start for University Hospital, Code 3.

****

The shooter, now about ten feet from me, looks up as I raise my gun and he raises his. My sights come into focus as his face blurs and his head becomes the size of a softball as my gun lines up with the center of his chest. My mind is blocking out everything around me. As I focus on the sights, I slowly squeeze the trigger. I feel the recoil of the pistol as my focus moves again to the shooter. I see his shirt jump just left of the button line, even with the top of the pocket, and his shoulder turn to the left and dip, as his head then turns to the left as if looking behind him. His left leg steps back to catch his balance, and his gun, still in both hands, falls to the left side of his chest.

My gun settles back from the recoil as I watch the man return to upright. His eyes are wide so that I can see white all the way around the brown center and his mouth opens in a silent scream. He takes a step forward and tries to raise the gun with both of his trembling hands. My focus returns to my sights as I squeeze the trigger for the second time and the recoil throws my gun up and to the right. Again, my eyes train on the target. I watch as his shirt this time jumps right on the button line, his shoulders roll forward and his head rotates towards his chest. His arms and legs move like a marionette with cut strings. As his head pivets back, his shoulders return to their post as his body falls straight back into the street.

I lower my gun to the ready and scan the area for a second target. Walking to the body to check for signs of life, I secure the shooters gun and say a prayer for his soul and mine. With my thumb and forefinger, I close his eyes.

From behind, I hear a voice yelling for me to drop the gun and get on my knees. I lay my gun on the ground. I stand and step back putting my hands behind my head. The voice again yells, "I said on your knees!" I lower myself to my knees and feel someone push me face first to the ground, while demanding, "Don't move." Another unseen person grabs my arm, forcing my hands behind my back, places cuffs on them and then pulls me to my feet. I'm looking at a kid, who may or may not be old enough to drink, poking me in my chest and demanding to know who I am.

Before I can answer, I hear someone yelling, "He's one of us, he's one of us!" The sergeant is running up the street waving his arms and shouting at the young agent that I'm a retired officer and to take the cuffs off. The little shit says he's sorry, but I'm sure he doesn't really mean it.

"That's okay. I'm just glad one of you school boys didn't shoot me once you came out of hiding. Does your mommy know you're playing police?"

The sergeant shakes his head reminding me to "play nice."

"Why? Really? I had to come out of retirement to do their job. Besides, who's gonna look after my friend that tried to tell them about the man with the gun?"

As I pick my gun up to return it to the holster, the agent tells me, "We'll need that."

"No, you don't. At least not until you get some help for my friend over there."

"You mean that drunk that's been bothering us all morning? EMS is working on him. He was just shot in the shoulder."

Stepping closer to look him in the eye, I fire back, "First, you immature brat, if you call him just a drunk again, EMS will be working on you! Got it? What he's been doing all morning is trying to tell you guys about the man with the gun. Had you listened, this wouldn't have happened. Now, I'm going over here and check on my friend and I'm gonna take my gun with me. Or, I could head over there to speak to my friends in the news, that what you want?" I take a breath. "Look, later I'll take my gun down to the state lab and have it test fired and then give it to the sergeant to put in the property room."

"But sir, we'll need the gun."

"I'll sell it to you."

"Damn Conway, just give him the damn gun."

"Okay, Sarge, here. I'm going to go check on the Colonel now."

 The agent looked at the sergeant and voices his opinion, "What an ass."

Smiling, the sergeant walks away, "Hell, you caught him on a good day, sonny."

The ER Will Never Be The Same

Hearing the Colonel voicing his displeasure at the top of his lungs about being shot, I'm pretty sure that he's going to be okay.

"Take him to University Hospital, not to VA. University is better with gunshots," I tell the EMT bandaging the Colonel's wound.

"We're headed there now. University is where they took the First Lady, sir."

"How do you know the First Lady was shot?"

"One of the reporters heard it on the police radio, it's already on the national news."

As they put the Colonel in the back of the truck I ask, "How's he doing?"

"I think he'll be fine. He wants a drink and a cheeseburger," the tech smiles, jumping into the drivers seat.

"Take good care of him."

"You want a ride?"

"I think I'm going to have to talk to the FBI."

"Okay. Sorry, but we got to go."

****

The quiet of the White House is broken as a Secret Service agent stops the secretary at the door as she tries to enter the oval office on a run. Joyce raises her head with tears in her eyes, and with a trembling voice quietly says, "The First Lady has been shot!"

"Where did you hear that?" asks the agent, still blocking the door with his broad shoulders and six foot two frame.

"It's on the news!"

"The President is meeting with his staff; you can't just pop in and yell that out."

"Why not?" Joyce challenged.

With that, the door opens and the Chief of Staff sticks his head out yelling, "Get Hamilton in here now!"

"Yes sir, Mr. Powers." The agent speaking into his radio calls for the Director of the Secret Service to the oval office asap.

Radio responds, "ETA five minutes."

"Sir, did you copy that?"

"Make it three," Carl Powers orders and disappears back behind the door.

Robert Hamilton still has his hand on the door when the President starts yelling, "How bad is she hurt and why didn't you tell me? Get the girls ready, we're going to Louisville."

"With all due respect Mr. President, what the hell are you talking about?"

"Lauren has been shot. I had to hear it on the news."

"I got the limo on the phone and the First Lady wasn't shot, it's Agent Martin."

"Does Agent Harris know?" asked Powers.

"Talk to me, Hamilton. Powers, call the girls back and tell them to unpack, we're not going to Louisville. Their mother wasn't shot, it was Agent Martin."

"Sir, Martin was shot in the hip, and a street person was also shot trying to stop the shooter. Both are going to be okay. The shooter was shot and killed by a retired local cop, the FBI is talking to him. Martin was protecting the First Lady and was taken, under her orders, to the hospital in the limo. Harris is with them."

"Get a female agent from Louisville to pack a bag, she'll be accompanying Lauren back and will be in Washington for a couple of weeks. And tell Harris to stay and look after Martin," orders the President, putting his cowboy boots on the yard sale coffee table that the First Lady had one of the housekeeping staff buy specifically for boots, so that he and the bunkhouse gang that works with him couldn't hurt the one that came in the oval office.

"What about the First Lady?"

"Tell her I love her and we'll see her when she gets back. She makes good choices. Besides, just because I can control the Armed Forces does not mean I can control her."

"Yes sir, I understand."

Tell The FBI What They Miss From 'Behind The Credentials'

Standing in the middle of the street watching the Secret Service and FBI trying to figure out who's going to take the fall for this mess, an agent who looks to me to be just another kid says, "Mr. Conway, I'm Agent Ryan and I need to take your statement, sir."

"If you can get me in the hospital to check on my friend, I'll answer your questions."

After a minute on the radio, he turns back to me, "You've been cleared to the hospital. You can ride with me."

Being stuck behind the police line, I can see the loading dock is overflowing with doctors and nurses. The police have cleared the press back as the limo pulls to a stop. The door flies open and two doctors that have been cleared by the Secret Service climb into the back seat. Agent Harris and the First lady exit the vehicle, both covered in blood, and are escorted into the hospital to the doctor's lounge, out of sight of the press. Agent Martin is placed on a gurney and rushed into room nine located deep inside the ER.

****

Live from the loading dock at the hospital, the local news reports, "The First Lady was able to walk into the ER from the limo." The fact there was another person shot in the limo went unnoticed.

EMS arrives with the Colonel, still looking for a drink and waving with his good arm at the crowd as he's wheeled into room nine and placed next to Martin. The assigned group of doctors and nurses move to the table and start removing his clothes. Agent Martin lays quiet on the gurney, the Colonel not so much. The doctor with the least amount of patience asked one of the nurses to shut him up. She smiles though her mask and says, "My pleasure," as she shoots something into his IV. In a couple minutes, it puts the Colonel on his back, awake but quiet.

Agent Davis enters the room just in front of me as Agent Ryan hands the First Lady a phone saying, "It's the President, ma'am."

"John, calm down, I'm all right. Agent Martin was shot and may be riding a desk for a while. The street guy that tried to stop the shooter is going to be all right and I would like to leave Harris here with Martin."

"Glad to hear everyone will be okay. There's an agent from Louisville who'll meet you at the plane and she knows she'll be in Washingston for a week or two. The girls know you're okay and they're standing right here. You want to say hi?"

"Of course I want to talk to my girls."

"Here, girls. I'm going back to work."

****

A short time later, the ER doctor steps in and speaks privately to the First Lady, but then stands back to include the whole room. "We're going to take both men to the OR and sew up their wounds. They'll be back in recovery in about an hour and then you can visit them in their rooms."

Once the doctor left, I'm left staring across the table at the kid agent. I'll bet his mother had to buy his first handgun. He reaches in his jacket pocket to pull out his official police notebook that came with his 'Batman secret decoder ring' and his 'Dick Tracy wrist radio'.

Polly and the First Lady are sitting in two easy chairs sipping soft drinks and laughing like schoolgirls, not at all like an FBI agent and the wife of the most powerful man in the free world.

Agent Ryan squares himself in his chair trying to look taller than his five foot seven inches and is doing his best to appear professional in front of the others and myself. In his deepest big boy voice, he asks if I had noticed the man with the gun before the shooting started. I can still hear the First Lady telling Polly how she met John, which seems to be a better story than the one I was reporting to Agent Ryan.

After an hour of Ryan asking, "And then what happened?" and hearing the worry in Polly's laugh while the First Lady attempted to keep the mood light, I'm relieved when the nurse steps in to tell us that Martin and the Colonel have been moved to their room and were ready for visitors. She leads us to a room with an agent standing outside the door holding a list of people allowed in. This agent is not a kid, but a six foot black man who was likely a linebacker in another life. He informs us that everyone has to sign in, even the First Lady. Showing him my ID card so he could check his list, I lean over and add my name to the paper on his clipboard.

Their hospital room is bright and noisy as nurses and doctors are hurrying around looking busy; checking and rechecking bandages, looking into eyes with their little lights and taking the blood pressure of most everyone in the room. I'm thinking they just want to be in the room with the Colonel and myself. Okay, maybe they want to be in the room with the First Lady.

The Colonel was in the bed next to the door and, through glassy eyes, waves at the First Lady as she pats him on the foot. With a big smile she leans in to tell him, "Thanks for what you did," as she passes by.

Polly was already at the bedside of Martin, checking on him with a kiss to his forehead.

With his eyes wide, Martin whispers, "What are you doing? The First Lady is watching."

"She knows Joey. Everybody knows."

"What?"

"It's all right. They've known for a while."

The First Lady steps up between the beds saying, "Just rest, Martin. Polly is going to stay in Louisville with you until you get out of the hospital. I've got to get back to the White House, my girls are having some issues and John is no good at telling them 'no'. If you two need anything at all, tell one of the agents and I'll see that you get it."

As she turns to leave, the Colonel says, "I could use a drink and a cheeseburger."

Everyone in the room laughs as the First Lady looks back over her shoulder, "I'll check with the nurses on my way out."

Most of the group leave the room, leaving only Harris and myself to say our goodbyes.

The Colonel looks up and says, "Who would ever think I'd be sharing a room with Aggie's boyfriend?"

"Who's Aggie?" Harris inquires, turning to look right at Martin.

"Don't know."

Before Martin gets shot again, I try to explain to Agent Harris about why we call Martin 'Aggie's boyfriend', and am rewarded with broad smiles on their faces.

As I tell the Colonel it's nine o'clock and there may be a shooting at my house, Agent Harris steps up to tell me she'll give me a ride. Thinking that likely won't help; gone all day, don't call, plus have a good looking young woman drop me off. Oh hell, why not?

A few minutes later as I trudge up the steps to the living room and inform Maureen I'm home, I find her watching television from my recliner, not looking amused. "I saw your picture on the news and your family keeps calling wanting to know if you're in jail. Was that your wino friend who got shot? Why didn't you call?"

"Yes, that was the Colonel who got shot, and he's doing okay, thanks for asking. What did the news say?"

"It showed the First Lady coming out of the mission, then your friend getting arrested, and then shot. Everyone is running, and the camera is waved all around. The next thing is another shot, then two more shots and a closeup of you kneeling over the body. Next, it shows you being arrested, pushed to the ground and cuffed."

"Well, they did turn me loose, but by that time social media was telling the world that the First Lady was shot and, like a swarm of bees, the reporters all left for the hospital. Sorry I didn't let you know what was going on, but it got busy and the FBI needed to talk."

"Call your sister," Maureen said, walking to the stairs to go on up to bed.

Waiting For The Colonel

The neighbors keep coming by until late and the phone rings until well past midnight. Bedtime is slow coming and lying in bed doesn't help sleep overtake me. Every time I close my eyes I relive the shooting, ending with me closing the shooter's eyes. I've seen the story on the news at least a dozen times, but now the news channels all want to interview me. I set up an appointment with a reporter I know and trust to interview the Colonel and myself, if the Colonel agrees.

After waiting for hours for the alarm to go off, I'm up before dawn to get things done around the house. Now with coffee ready, clothes in the wash, dishes done, bed made and Maureen off to work, I walk down to the Y to work out and talk to the flower children, while I wait for McDonald's to stop serving breakfast.

An hour or so later, I stop by the condo for a quick shower and then go downstairs to back the car out of the garage. McDonalds is on the corner, but the hospital is about two miles away and that's a long way to carry five coffees and a bag of dumpster burgers.

Pulling to the back of the parking lot near the dumpster, I find that one of the Colonel's colleagues has already been in the dumpster digging out all the Egg McMuffins.

When I ask him how many he has, he answers, "Eight. Why?"

"I'll give you five dollars for the whole bag."

"Give me the money first."

I give him the money, then go though the drive-thru for five cups of black coffee.

After parking in the garage across the street from the hospital, I cross the street and ride the elevator to the Colonel's third floor room, just across from the nurse's station. Finding no agent standing outside, I push the door open to find him standing just inside.

Agent Harris is sitting in the chair next to Martin's bed, with her feet propped up next to his. She asks me to sign in and points at the list, lying on a counter near the door. The Colonel is entertaining the room, including the nurses as they come and go, with stories from the alleys and the abandoned buildings he calls home. I pull over a chair as he finishes a story about getting the rats drunk on wine and watching them try to get back in their respective holes in the wall. By this point, he has Harris referring to Martin as Aggie's boyfriend.

"I've got dumpster burgers and coffee for anyone who wants them."

"I want some. Did you get them at 2nd and Broadway? They have the best," the Colonel speaks up.

"I'll have one and a cup of coffee please," Harris speaks up.

"Me too," said Martin, "They gotta be better than this hospital food."

I hand two to the agent at the door, along with a cup of black coffee. "You may want to put them in the microwave, they've been off the grill for awhile," I give him a sly smile.

As one of the morning staff nurses comes in, the agent at the door puts his Egg McMuffin down to check her ID and have her sign in. Martin finishes his in three bites and the Colonel is on his second one. Harris is half finished, when the agent at the door, starting his second one remarks, "There's coffee grounds on my burger. Where did you get these?"

With a mouthful of burger, the Colonel announces, "The dumpster behind Mickey D's. Don't you school boys know what a dumpster burger is?"

Martin and the Colonel continue eating, but Harris' mind is winning over her stomach as she moves toward the trash can in the corner. The agent at the door, with his red hair and now green face, is beginning to look a bit like Christmas.

Once things settle down and everyone is drinking their coffee and returning to their normal color, I ask the Colonel if he wanted me to get in touch with his family. Harris, still staring at me and hoping that I was lying about the dumpster, tells us that the First Lady had the FBI checking on that.

"You don't need to go to any trouble, I blew it years ago," the Colonel says, looking sad briefly, but then finishing his coffee while reaching for another burger.

"Well, they found them in the waiting room of the hospital checking on you. Seems you're a pain in the ass, but you're still family and they're worried about you. You need to see them. They're waiting for me to let them know when to come in, what should I tell them?" Agent Harris says, still not getting too far from the trash can.

"Tell them yes, I'd like to see them."

"How about around lunch time? I'll walk Joey to the cafeteria so you guys can have the room."

"Thanks, that'd be great."

"Good, I've already checked with the nurse to set it up. Of course, that was before you and your sick friend told us that you fed us food from a dumpster," Harris grumbles, still trying to convince herself that breakfast didn't really come out of the trash.

"I'll get on out of here, you know how to get hold of me when you get out or need something. We've still got stories to tell and questions to answer," I remind the Colonel as I move towards the door.

"Wait, Conway. You stay. I want you here when my sister gets here."

"You scared of her?"

"Yes."

It was then that the door opens, and the room is filled with little girls. Actually, there were only two, but the noise equaled that of at least a dozen. The first one to appear was about three feet tall with the big brown eyes of a puppy dog and a giant pink bow taming her dark brown curls. Being too young to know her Great-Uncle Roger, due to his exile into the street from the family, she bursts through the door, touching everything and asking, "What's this?" The other little beauty holding onto her daddy's finger and obviously just learning to walk, has big blue eyes and blond hair, what there is of it. She escapes his hold and immediately starts climbing onto the bed to reach the Colonel. A beautiful woman, much younger than I had expected, is only steps behind followed by a middle-aged couple.

The Colonel, looking up with a smile on his face says, "These two rowdies are my great-nieces. Older one is Mary and this little one is Linda. The lady trying to control them is my niece, Robin, and that's her husband, Dave. This lady is my sister Deana, and he's my brother-in-law, Rick."

After the introductions, Harris and Martin move to the door and inform the room they're going to the lunchroom to get coffee. The Colonel reminds them to check and see if they have dumpster burgers down there. Harris stops long enough to ask, "Those burgers didn't really come from a dumpster did they? No, never mind. I don't want to know."

"What's a dumpster burger, Uncle Roger?" asks Robin.

"Long story, Pumpkin. I'll tell you later."

Deana starts in with, "When I saw you get shot on TV, it looked like it was the police who shot you."

"I'd been trying to tell them the guy had a gun, and I heard him say he was going to shoot the First Lady. They wouldn't listen to me, so when they had me in handcuffs and I saw him pull the gun, I had no other choice but to break free and run at him."

"Who's the man in the corner?" Robin asks him, looking in my direction.

"That's the guy who shot the man after he shot me. He's retired Detective Conway and my friend."

"Nice to meet y'all," I speak up, attempting to stay hidden in the corner.

"Well, we need to get the girls out of here before they break something, but we'll be here to pick you up tomorrow morning when you get discharged," insists Deana.

"You don't have to do that. I can stay at the mission."

"You're coming to stay with us, at least until you recover," she leans over and kisses him on the cheek with a 'don't argue with me' expression on her face.

As the door closes behind them, we can hear the girls going down the hall telling everyone they passed and the nurses at the station "Bye-bye" accompanied with sweet little girl smiles. The room seems empty, now void of their loud energy.

The Colonel climbs out of bed and pulls up a chair facing me, with our knees touching. With tears in his eyes, he first looks at the floor and slowly raises his head to look in my eyes as he whispers, "I just can't stay at their house."

"Why? I think they love you and are willing to give you another chance. Besides, those two girls need a great-uncle to teach them things only a great-uncle can teach."

"It's not that. They've made me an apartment in the basement; complete with a bedroom, sitting room, kitchen and bath."

"Well, that sounds terrible."

"Have you ever had a boogie man under the bed or in the closet when you were little, after the lights were turned out?"

"Sure, every kid has known a boogie man, it's what sells night lights."

"Did the night light make the boogie man go away?"

"No, you still see them in the shadows," I say, remembering.

"Did your mom and dad tell you that there was nothing in the closet or under the bed?"

"Sure, sometimes they'd shine a flashlight and show me under the bed and in the closet."

"Well, the basement is like a bunker when the lights go out and my boogie man is the war. I can hear the bad guys tiptoeing though the wire. When you put a night light on, you see the shadows coming though the wire and every sound is the war getting closer."

"Have you talked to anybody about it?" I ask.

"I'm a grown man. I should know there's no Santa Claus, Easter bunny or boogie man. I don't want to let people know I'm scared of the dark."

"I know we've already been down this road, but go to the VA and get some help. That's what they're there for."

"You ever been to the VA?" snapped the Colonel.

"No. I've always had good insurance, so I go to the hospital."

"Well, let me just remind you what you get. You get to fill out pages and pages of paperwork. Then you're told that you have an appointment in thirty days, with a doctor or a group leader who has never even fired a shot in anger, much less been shot at." The Colonel's face was grim.

"But, they are educated to handle the problems you have."

"After the session, the vets get together over a beer or a drink and talk about what a waste of time it was and how little the person leading the group knows about what they're going through."

"Well, if you tell your sister about the basement and that you can't stay there, maybe they can work something out."

"Hey, what the hell! We got stories to tell and dumpster burgers to eat," the Colonel shrugs and leans back, smiling that nervous smile again.

"Yes, and you have memories yet to make with those two little girls and more good memories to make with your family. It's time you came home from the war and left the boogie man behind." I give him an encouraging smile and step out of the door, but my mind is racing as I walk down the hallway from the Colonel's room. "Would I ever see him again? Would he stay on the wagon? Would he get over coming home from the war when so many of his friends didn't?"

Looking back over my shoulder I smile because deep in my heart I know there's stolen breakfasts to be had at the hotel and dumpster burgers to be eaten with my hero. The real question is what to do with my morning until he calls.

The Colonel Returns

A couple weeks after the shooting, I hear that Martin and Harris are back in Washington. The First Lady will take care of them and no one will be surprised if there's not a little agent running around the White House in a year or two. I know the Colonel and I could have made real street cops out of them if we'd had the time. Dumpster burgers and cheap wine right out of the bottle on a cold night around a fire barrel classroom would get them right up to snuff. Right now though I'm missing the Colonel, his stories, and having someone to get in trouble with. I head over toward the bus stop, but I know that having coffee there just wouldn't be the same. It's just a bus stop, not a time machine or a liar's bench.

The young lady in the coffee shop said she'd seen me on television and had been telling everybody that she had served coffee to the Colonel and me a couple days before the shooting. "Where is the old guy? I saw him get shot. He's not dead is he?" With a smile to show that I appreciate her concern, I answer, "No, he's recovering at his sister's."

Walking away, she laughs over her shoulder, "I remember when you guys first came in. The manager almost had a litter of kittens."

I thank her and start for home, wondering what boring things I'll do today to kill time until Maureen gets home from work. There are only so many times you can wax the floor, run the vacuum or dust. After listening to the Colonel's version of *As the World Turns*, house cleaning just doesn't fill my needs. After a trip back into the war, breaking up a robbery and a shootout saving the First Lady, who wants to go back to dusting and making the bed? I had the voices in my head working on the problem as I walked; should I take my nap in my easy chair or on the sofa? Decisions, decisions.

My cell phone rings from the depths of my pocket and I check caller ID. The number is unknown to me and I'm sure that a nap is going to win over buying whatever these people are selling. But, I still have a couple blocks to walk home so I answer, "Conway".

A voice as soothing as pea gravel being dumped in a coal bucket comes from my phone and barks in my ear, "Well, I'm glad to hear you're not dead or in jail without me to watch out for you."

"It's about time you called. I was thinking you didn't love me anymore."

"My sister watches me close and I haven't had a dumpster burger or a drink since the shooting. Her liquor cabinet is empty as last year's campaign promises," the Colonel's laughs turns into a plea, "Come get me."

"I can do that. Where are you?"

"You know where Prospect is?"

"I know, but I'm pretty sure they don't let winos out there."

I hear the smile in the Colonels voice, "I'll put in a good word for you. Come out Brownsboro Road until it becomes Highway 22. Look for a gate that says Rolling Hills Farm, turn in and I'll be waiting."

"Give me thirty minutes."

I jog home to get my car. It's Colonel 'story time'.

Twenty minutes later, excitement mounts as I turn through a stone gate under a swinging 'Rolling Hills Farm' sign. A white fence spans the yard and driveway for a half mile, then continues though tall hundred-year-old oak trees and then forks. One way leads towards four horse barns with red roofs and a steeple on each end. The other fork ends at a circular drive in front of a two-story white frame house with a wrap-around porch. Gingerbread trim decorates the exterior, going all the way around the old southern style home.

I spy the Colonel sitting in a rope swing, hanging from the limb of a gnarled old tree.

"Well, nice house. Your sister's place?"

The Colonel pulls himself up out of the swing, wearing tan slacks and a blue oxford cloth dress shirt tucked in, brown penny loafers with a belt to match and no socks.

"Is now," he says, climbing in the passenger seat.

"What do you mean, 'is now'?"

"Let's get lunch and I'll tell you the whole story. You won't get off my back until I do."

"This place is so big it has its own zip code," I smile, turning the car around and heading back down the long driveway.

"Let's go someplace nice. My sister is buying just to get me out of the house."

"How about Famous David's Bar-B-Q? You up for that?"

"You're driving and Sis is buying. I can eat anything."

Pulling out onto the two lane, I can't wait and I poke him in the arm with my finger.

"So what's the story?"

The Colonel stares out the window with a troubled look as the next few miles go by, not speaking and breathing shallow. Finally, bringing himself back to the present, he answers, "Okay, but I get a beer with my lunch. I guess I should start at the beginning."

"I thought that was where we started the first time we met?" I'm watching out the windshield, but wanting to look him in the eye to see if he's really back in present time.

"My story starts in college before the Army. Dad was looking for me to go to college and then into the family business. I went to school, but not to class. Stayed drunk and partied the whole first year. Then grades came out and, I was told not to come back. My GPA was 0.0. Dad called in as many favors as he could, but I got a letter from Uncle Sam, anyway. Now, when do I hear about what makes you who you are? Bet you have stories for the bus stop bench."

"What do you want to know? Wait, I'm not the one scared to sleep in the basement because of the boogie man," I tease, trying to manuever a smile out of him.

"So you say."

After pulling in the parking lot, I lock the car and put the keys in my pocket. Hurrying, I try to catch up with the Colonel as he strides ascross the lot toward the restaurant. "Let's eat first, then go to the liar's bench for coffee and life stories."

"Well, what do we talk about at lunch?"

"How about that big ass house and farm you decided to drink out of your life?"

"That's a story for the bench, first about you," he shakes his head, still a few steps ahead and not slowing down as we walk in the door. The restaurant's full of the lunchtime crowd with the overflow seated in the bar. We settle at a table there and each of us reaches for a menu.

A waitress appears at our table, ready to take our drink order and I'm grateful that she buys me some time. Not waiting to be asked, the Colonel glances at her and proceeds to order, "Two light beers and potato skins. We'll live it up, Sis is buying."

Taking a deep breath, I begin; "I was born here in Louisville and other than the time in the Marines, I've always lived here. Got out of high school and couldn't wait to leave home, so I joined the service and was gone by summer's end. Then boot camp, a trip to the war and back to the states to wander from school to school for the rest of my enlistment."

The waitress brings our beer and potato skins and takes our food order. We eat, discuss the weather, the people in the bar and other general small talk. I know that when we're done eating, I'm going to have to tell my story.

Back To The Liar's Bench

Full of pulled chicken barbecue and potato skins, we head out to the car for the ride downtown to Second and Jefferson and the bus stop. I'm not sure why, but I feel better talking at the bus stop and I think the Colonel does too.

On the way, I tell the Colonel I wasn't a drinker before going into the military, just never had the money to party like that. Had to borrow the family car and have it home by midnight. Putting gas in the car and paying for a movie· or dinner was the end of a week's salary.

"You're the second poor dumb boy that went in the Corps, is that a requirement?" the Colonel asks with that faraway look on his face again.

"You have friends that went into the marines?" I ask hoping for one of his smart-ass answers. All I get is silence as the Colonel stares out the window as if he could see a hundred miles ahead. We don't talk the rest of the way downtown.

Once I park the car and get out, I suggest we get coffee and then go to the bench. He nods and we walk in the front door of the coffee shop as if we own the place and not one person stops to stare.

The coffee shop only has one other customer and the college girl who works the morning shift is getting off. She's out of her uniform, wearing tight jeans and a green sweatshirt with the Jets team logo on the front. She drops her backpack full of school books and hugs the Colonel, then me. "I'm so glad to see you're all right," she announces, hugging the Colonel a second time.

"Thank you young lady, for thinking of me and the hug for an old man." the mood of the Colonel lightens for a minute.

"These are the men who saved the First Lady," she yells to an almost empty coffee shop.

Once she's off to school and we have our coffee in hand, we cross the street to the bus stop where the liar's bench is empty. The Colonel and I both sit and lean back against the plexiglass and take a thoughtful sip from our cups.

"Well, should we start with the big farm, the reason that you stared out the window all the way down here, or your Marine friend?" I ask, trying to get the party started.

The Colonel never opens his eyes, just takes another sip and starts to talk, almost like he's talking to someone only he can see. "The morning was rainy, and I was scared. It was my first mission in the field outside the control of the trainers and my mom was talking in my head 'It's all fun and games until someone loses an eye'. From the time the sergeant had briefed us until we loaded the choppers, I wished I'd taken the training more seriously. Our job was to help clear the many ridges that run down from the top of Hill 881."

The Colonel leans forward with his elbows on his knees and opens his eyes, lost in the past. In his mind's eye, he's back on Hill 881. He's shaking and tears streak his cheeks. "The choppers let us out five or so feet off the ground. As soon as we exit the aircraft, someone starts firing at us. We run for the tree line and cover, slipping and sliding in the mud. I end up in the jungle underbrush. The rain clouds and the jungle block the sun, making it dark as night. After a head-over-heels tour of the hill, I can only feel around for my helmet and weapon."

When he stops talking, I ask the Colonel if he's okay and he looks at me like he is seeing me for the first time. "You sure you're okay, Colonel?"

"Sure, I'm okay. Just remembering, that's all."

I smile and stand up. "Save my seat, I'll get us refills."

Crossing the street and back, I return in less than five minutes. The Colonel is gone. I sit down in hopes that he just went to piss and will be right back.

After about ten minutes, I start worrying that one of his street buddies has come by and he's fallen off the wagon. As I'm trying to work out what I'm going to tell his sister, he reappears with pie, smiling that sort of smile a kid gives when he knows he's worried you and he may be in trouble.

"I was thinking that a piece of pie would go good with our coffee on top of the Bar-B-Q," the Colonel says, holding out a pie from the pie kitchen a block over.

"A whole pie?"

"Hey, I know some guys that'll eat it with some wine," laughs the Colonel, pulling out a couple paper plates and forks.

Settling back on the bench with my coffee and pie, I ask, "What happened on that hill?"

"First our pie and coffee. The story will come in its own time. Tell me about you."

"After boot camp, I came home for leave before being assigned to a unit, first California and then Vietnam. We got off the plane and checked in. The next morning, after breakfast, we fall in and they start down the line, assigning people to different units. When they were done, there was maybe twenty of us left and a sergeant came up and told us to get on the trucks near the mess tent. We were going to recon. Once at the unit, I was assigned to a fourteen-man team. The team leader's name was Scott, who told us there was only one way to get into a team and that was to replace someone who had got killed. Most of these guys had been together in the team since recon school and for the first two or three hours, no one talked to me. I was afraid it would be a long tour of duty, but suddenly Scott remembered that I was from Kentucky and a Louisville fan. One of the guys at the far end of the tent yelled, "Go Cards!" and just like that, I was a member of the team.

"You Marines are sure a close knit group. If you didn't go to Parris Island, you're not a real warrior," says the Colonel, chasing his last piece of pie with a gulp of black coffee.

"That's right, soldier. Now, tell me all about the farm."

"The farm is the end of the story that started on the hill," the look the Colonel gives me lets me know he believes my motives are good.

"If talking about it helps, I'm here for you. I'm not a doctor, but I'll listen."

"I know, but unlike the kids they hire as doctors these days, you've been there. You understand," the Colonel say, looking around for his coffee.

Then, looking back at me, he says, "You want to get a couple bottles of wine and take the rest of the pie out to the wino-camp? Or are you scared?"

The Wino Encampment

Climbing in my car and closing the driver's door, I ask if we should stop by the Walgreen's to pick up some wine before we go to the camp. The Colonel laughs out loud. I'm guessing he's amused at me thinking the wine at the drugstore would be what street people would buy.

"Can you see these guys putting a handful of coins on the counter at the local Walgreen's and asking for a nice white table wine that would go with grilled fish and asparagus?" he howls, hitting the dashboard with the palms of his hands as he continues to be entertained at my ignorance.

"Okay, wino connoisseur. Where do we go?" I ask, as his laughter begins to subside.

"The nine hundred block of Market Street. There's a liquor store on the corner."

I pull up in front of a blue filling station turned liquor store, with a drive-thru window. The pumps are gone, but the overhang is still there and the name of the service station can still be seen from where the letters were removed, but never painted over. The new owner had spared no expense, using a three-inch paintbrush and a quart of black paint free handing the words 'Liquor Store' on both sides. Walking inside is even more of a flashback to the days when I was a cop on the beat.

Once in the door, we were in a six-by-six foot room surrounded on three sides by counters of wood paneling and bullet proof glass reaching to the ceiling. Opposite the door, there are holes drilled in the glass so the patrons can order and then recover their requests from a slot cut in the counter that can only be opened on one side at a time.

A bell rings when the door is opened and bangs against it. This summons the voice of an unpleasant man who would rather be home with a drink of his own, "What do you want?"

"Two Bottles of Night Train," the Colonel barks back.

"Pints or fifths?"

"Fifths," yells the Colonel as if the man wouldn't be able to hear though the little holes.

"Three dollars. Let me see your money."

Reaching into my pocket I ask, "Is that three dollars apiece?"

The Colonel smiles, shakes his head and says, "No, that's the total."

Sliding a five dollar bill in the drawer, I watch as it closes and then opens again with the two bottles of wine and two dollars in change.

Taking the bottles and the money, I look up into the hard eyes of the man as he says instead of thank you, "Something else?"

"Nope," I mumble as he walks away.

Returning to the car I ask, "Why the Night Train, besides the price?"

"More alcohol per volume and the price is right. If you're a drunk, it's all you want."

"Well, everything goes good with dumpster burgers," I laugh at my own joke.

I follow the Colonel's directions to the camp and pull into the blacktop lot of the park near the river, just west of the Nugent Sand Company. The path we take from the car is between the tree line and the four-story high piles of sand and gravel that's been dredged from the Ohio River. On the bank of the river, before it starts down the hill to the waterline, we find a campfire, a tent and several lean-tos. The Colonel calls to a man with his back to us, facing the fire.

"This is Seven Eleven," the Colonel says as the guy, looking to be in his late fifties and wearing jeans, a wool shirt and glasses with thick plastic frames, stands to shake hands. He's holding a can of something that had been sitting in the fire cooking and has the label burned off. The top is bent back, making a handle.

"Is Seven Eleven the unit he was in while in the army?" I ask the Colonel.

"Nope, we call him that because his mouth is always open."

"We brought wine and pie," I announce, not knowing what else to say.

"And a cop too," a woman's voice spits from behind a tree.

"That pretty lady is Maggie Jones. She's our very own queen of the street people," Seven Eleven fills me in.

"She has a mouth like a sailor and it doesn't get better when she's drunk," the Colonel adds.

Maggie is five feet of skin and bones wearing a tee shirt, bib overalls and high top black tennis shoes. Topping a prunish looking face, her salt and pepper hair is short and curly. On the rare occasion that she smiles, you can see that the alcohol and the street have taken most of her teeth.

It wasn't necessary for the Colonel or Seven Eleven to introduce me to Maggie as I had arrested her before on many occasions. When she begged for money, she'd curse the people who passed by without giving her any and if she'd been drinking, she'd try to fight everybody, including the police. Maggie and I had some real scuffles in the past, trying to get her in the back of my police car.

"Why did you bring Conway to the encampment?" growls Maggie.

"He's Detective Conway, and he's retired," the Colonel speaks up. "Besides, he paid for the wine."

"How many people live here?" I ask the group as we pull up logs and buckets to sit around the fire.

Maggie, still having some trust issues, answers, "Sometimes ten or twelve, but right now four.

Seeing that Seven Eleven is cooking brown beans in his can, I ask if they get food from the mission, which makes everybody laugh.

"Sure, we get it from the mission people and from the churches and businesses bringing boxes of food. Sometimes, they leave them on the loading dock at night and we steal a case or two of whatever's there," the Colonel explains, "This is what we eat here, but we go to the mission for lunch."

"So, I guess that frees up the money you beg on the street for booze?"

Seven Eleven looks up from his beans, "We go on Friday and Saturday nights to hang out near the liquor stores where the kids buy their drinks for the night. We buy their beer or whiskey for them, but whatever they buy for themselves they also have to buy for us."

"Don't the shopkeepers question you?" I ask, rubbing my head and watching, as Maggie digs out some pie with her fingers.

"We buy warm beer by the case. The kids know to bring a cooler and it's easier for us to store," Seven Eleven answers, as he throws his empty bean can into a pile under a tree.

"You drink hot beer?" I question, wishing I had a fork or at least a washrag to give Maggie.

"We may be drunks and can't keep a job, but we're not dumb," I'm informed by Maggie, her face covered with pie, reminding me of a two-year-old.

"Over on the Hay Market, the shops that sell and buy goods off their loading docks keep CO_2 fire extinguishers out there. One will cool a dozen cases of beer," the Colonel says.

I walk away to phone Maureen and tell her I'm going to have supper with the Colonel. I don't, however, tell her we've been out most of the day or that we're eating beans in the wino camp down by the river.

Seven Eleven throws a log on the fire and Maggie gets us each a can of beans and the can opener. I'm not sure how this boney little woman could be hungry after just eating half of a cherry pie, some of which can still be seen lingering on her face.

The cans are opened and set in the fire pit on the coals. We sit back to wait as Seven Eleven says, "Let me tell you about the first time I met Conway."

Let The Stories Begin

Maggie hands out hobo flatware, it's the Wendy's pattern tonight and still in it's wrap, thank goodness. Then, sitting a Mickey D's bag full of Taco Bell condiments down near the group, she announces that she wants to tell her story first.

The Colonel shows me how to take a third of the beans out and throw them in the fire, watching not to lose the juice because that's what the beans will cook in, and then stir in Taco Bell sauce to taste. Maggie and Seven Eleven are in the bag 'Like a duck on a June bug' as my daddy would say.

Waiting for the dust to settle, I look around. The sun is setting and the light coming though the trees spotlights a rickety chair propped next to a tree, missing its right rear leg. A large black and brown striped cat, weighing maybe fifteen to twenty pounds, leaks off its sides as it finishes off a field mouse and pushes the remains off the chair with it's paw. Then, with it's front two paws distending, head down and rear end up, the large feline makes a slow cat stretch, ending with two or three circles in the chair before settling down.

The Colonel turns in my direction and suggests, "Break out one of the bottles of wine."

Seven Eleven and Maggie stop pawing through the condiments as soon as the word "wine" comes out of the Colonel's mouth.

The Colonel winks and says, "Your wine, you take the first drink."

Unscrewing the cap, I take a drink of the dark thick wine, then pass the bottle to the Colonel and he turns it up. From where I am sitting, I can see him use his tongue as a stopper and not drink a drop. The bottle passes to

Maggie, who drinks a cup or so before Seven Eleven grabs it from her.

"You gonna drink it all?" barks Seven Eleven.

"It ain't your wine," snaps Maggie.

"Well, you asked how somebody could get killed at the fire barrel," smiles the Colonel.

"I'm gonna tell you about the first time I met Conway!" Maggie yells, grabbing the bottle back.

"Looks like we're out of the drinking loop," laughs the Colonel.

"I'm sure you don't remember the first time you met me, you were too drunk," I laugh.

"I do too! It was at the bus station and I was asking people for money. Somebody there called the cops. You came and told me I had to leave and I got mad and started cussing. You locked me up."

"It was snowing out, the jail was warm and dry and you needed a place to sleep off your drunk. But that wasn't the first time we met," I correct her. Finishing my beans and throwing my can in the pile, I continue, "You were so drunk you had no idea who we were or where you were. It was at Third and Market and you were lying on your back with your leg stuck in a storm drain. The people in the store had tried to help you, but you cussed and swung at them. The fire department, EMS, and the police all came. Your foot was stuck between the bars in the drain cover all the way to your knee. When the firemen tried to free you, you kicked them with your free foot and tried to bite them. Finally, we put a spit mask over your head so you couldn't bite and used gauze to tie your arms down at your sides. Then, one of the firemen and I held you down with a long bar from the fire truck across your shoulders while the EMS people put oil on your leg to get you free."

By now the first bottle is long gone, Seven Eleven and Maggie are well into the second one and Maggie has fallen backwards off her bucket for the third time. Both Maggie and Seven Eleven are now falling down drunk on less than a bottle of wine each.

"Was Maggie stuck in the storm drain your funniest drunk story?" the Colonel asks, helping Maggie back on her bucket.

"Oh no, not by a long shot. The funniest story I remember happened in the winter around Christmas."

"Can't wait to hear this one," he says eager for me to share.

"In the colder months, when the temperature gets below freezing, the city sends out a memo to watch out for the homeless so they don't freeze in an alley or an abandoned building. Around nine o'clock on a night when it was probably 15 degrees, we got a call to check on a man down in the 1400 block of Fourth Street. This area isn't known for its compassion, so we know this person is on the sidewalk in front of somebody's house and they are more interested in having the guy moved out of sight than in his health or well-being. When I got there, I recognize the subject on the street and so does the other officer who pulls up behind me. It was No-Toes Tyler. We called him that because he had passed out in an freezing cold alley behind a dumpster while hiding from the mission people, who were trying to get the homeless population inside and out of the weather. By the time the police found him, he had frostbite of his toes so bad they had to be amputated. Now he stuffs restaurant napkins in the toes of his shoes so they don't turn up and I think it probably helps balance him so he can walk. The other officer and I tried to get him off the cold ground and put him in the car so he can warm up. When we tried to help him up, he screamed and yelled that we were hurting him. Thinking he may have injured himself when he fell, we waited for EMS so we wouldn't do more damage. When EMS got there, they recognize No-Toes too. They checked him out in hopes he didn't want to go to the hospital because they don't want to put him in their truck. When they try to stand him up, he starts yelling again, so they lay him back down to finish checking him out. All of a sudden the EMS tech started laughing, "He peed his pants and froze to the sidewalk!"

The joke was on them because once they got him unstuck, they had to transport him."

By now, the fire had died down and Seven Eleven and Maggie were passed out. Looking at my watch, I see it's almost eight thirty and I still have to take the Colonel home. Maybe now he'll be in the mood to talk about what happened on the hill.

The Colonel To The Rescue

The Colonel finds some covers for Seven Eleven and Maggie as I check to make sure the fire is safe. Maggie has fallen sideways after passing out, leaving her left leg on top of the bucket with the rest of her body on the ground. I put her leg on the ground and place the bucket between her and the fire pit in hopes that she won't roll over into the fire, and then cover her to protect her from the dew. The Colonel covers Seven Eleven, who's curled up next to a tree looking a lot like the cat. With the light from the moon and the two floodlights over the large belts high in the air used to move the sand, we find the path back to my car. From behind a pile of sand, a huge "something" steps in front of us. All I can think is, "No wonder they can't find Sasquatch in the great north woods, he's right here on River Road in Louisville."

"Big Charlie! Where you been? Conway, this is Charlie," the Colonel smiles and introduces me to his big buddy.

I put my hand out to shake Charlie's and it disappears to my elbow in his large paw. Big Charlie is about six foot six and a wall of muscle. The shirt he's wearing has enough cloth to re-canvas Old Iron Sides. I sense he's a little slow in the head, just a large kid, mentally maybe fourth grade level.

"I've been working at the Hay Market, cleaning up after the trucks are unloaded. Got twenty-five dollars! I got to keep fifteen after I paid for my insurance," Charlie grins, holding up a ten and a five.

"Who did you give ten dollars to for your insurance?" asks the Colonel, shooting a glance at me.

"The truck driver said I had to have insurance to work on the truck in case I got hurt. But I didn't," Charlie smiles.

"You get some rest Charlie, another work day tomorrow," the Colonel says caringly, but I notice that his smile is gone.

"Nice meeting you, Charlie," I say walking away, glad that he's friendly.

On the way back to the car, the Colonel has his head down, grumbling to himself and getting madder with every step. I know he's thinking about the driver taking advantage of Charlie and wondering how many times he had done it in the past. In the back of my mind, I'm also planning how we could get this fine person just what he has coming.

Back at the car, the Colonel climbs in and closes the door. Staring out the windshield, he mumbles in a voice I had never heard coming from him, "We're gonna get that asshole!"

"We?" I ask, trying to keep him from knowing I was thinking the same thing myself.

"Yes, we. You got a problem with that?"

"No. Just let me think what he can be charged with and how we can catch him."

The rest of the ride home passes with small talk about the camp and the bean supper. I ask him why he didn't take a drink of the wine and he tells me he's scared that he might be an alcoholic, and has promised his sister he wouldn't drink. We talked about the two little girls that called him Uncle Roger and the joy they bring to his heart.

"I wish I hadn't wasted all that time, I missed so much." I'm not sure the Colonel even realizes he's said that out loud. He talks about being a pony for rides around the living room, tea parties for hours and making sure there are always boxes of raisins in his pocket for treats. He must spend every penny he has on those little girls. As I drop him off, we make plans to meet for lunch and talk about how to handle the truck driver.

I toss and turn through another sleepless night, thinking about the truck driver. My plan is to take the Colonel downtown to the robbery office the next day and see what kind of help we can muster up.

****

By morning, I decide to go by myself and talk to them before picking him up, but the minute I reach the office door I know something is wrong.

"What's going on?" I ask from the door.

A shiny new detective stands up and I recall working with him when he was on the street. Andrew Schneider was the name I read on his desk nameplate, but I know that his grandfather and myself are the only people who call him Andy. He has a sucker in his mouth as if he's just given up smoking, but he really just has a sweet tooth. Caramels, mints and suckers stick out of his coat pocket, candy bars live in his briefcase and in the glove box of his car, and stacks of cupcakes and Ho Ho's are on display in his partially opened desk drawer.

People underestimate this young man's skills and intelligence because of his easygoing nature and the slow gait of his speech. But, it's a definite mistake to sell him short.

In an office that should be empty during court and breakfast time, I'm surprised to find it full of detectives, commanding officers, TV cameras and print reporters. I suspect I should have watched the news this morning.

Working my way around the group using the 'cockroach method', I scoot against the wall, trying not to knock off any of the photos or plaques.

"What's going on, Andy?" I whisper, so as to not invite anyone else into the conversation.

"Let's go downstairs for coffee, it's a long story," Andy grins.

Getting on the elevator as more reporters are pouring out, we ride alone to the break room in the basement.

****

Andy starts the story of the way his workday had begun, "You know the spot where the city stores salt for icy roads, and cops on late watch go sometime to eat pizza and talk on slow nights?"

"Sure. I've spent a night or two there myself," I remember out loud.

"Well, last night there was a choir practice. Isn't that what you old guys called it when you got together for beer? Well, there was one down there. After they left, a homeless person checked for any pizza left over in the boxes they discarded, and found a body." Andy nods in a way that tells me there's more to the story.

"So, what's got the brass and the news out before breakfast?"

"The homeless person was Maggie. She told the lady at the mission, who called the police. Now we can't find Maggie and none of the street people will talk to us. The body had to be there before the police got together because it was covered in pizza boxes and beer cans. The news people are yelling about the police ignoring a body and asking if they might have been drunk. ETU had to take pictures of the scene, but the boxes and everything else was picked up before the reporters were let in. They all think we're covering something up. We need to talk to the winos about what they know.

Smiling into my coffee cup and not looking up at Andy, I said, "I may know someone who can help."

"You know a 'wino whisperer'?" Andy chuckles, dropping his half-full coffee cup in the trash. "I got to get back upstairs."

"I have someone who can get the street people to talk with you. Just you. You in?" I ask, stopping him in his tracks.

You Help Me, I'll Help You

All the way to the Colonel's house, I'm going over in my head how I'm going to convince the Colonel to help with the pizza killing, when all he wants is to get the truck driver. Did he not tell me, and I quote, "I know some cops too, but I don't tell them shit"?

Pulling up to the front of the farmhouse, I see the Colonel on the porch with both little girls. "Let me put the girls in the house, be right back," the Colonel yells, jumping up and herding the girls into the house.

Almost at a run, he takes his seat in the car and starts talking, "Did you come up with a way to get that truck driver?"

"First, I got something I want to ask you. The police have a problem we can help them with and in turn they'll help us."

"What do you mean we can help? I don't help the cops."

"We're going down to police headquarters to meet a guy I think you'll like. Once we set the ground rules for both cases, I'll let you tell him about the truck driver and what we need done."

I pull the car into a spot on the street in front of police headquarters and call Andy to ask him to meet us downstairs in the break room and to come alone.

When I hang up the phone, the Colonel grins and tells me that I sound like something out of a really old, really bad movie. Laughing, we both get out of the car and the Colonel starts for the front door. I grab him by the arm saying, "Let's go in the back door though the garage. It'll cut down on the number of cops that see us before we get a deal."

I punch in the code numbers, the overhead door rolls up, and we walk into a long dark driveway. The dark adds to the dirty look of the drive, which is wide enough for a lane in both directions. At the far end are eight parking spaces for the staff officers. Halfway down on the left are two elevators with dark green doors and a call button in between. Just a few feet past the elevators is a blue door with six inch white block letters spelling ETU. No window, just a door bell and speaker. Straight across the driveway is a dark brown door, that seems to never have been closed, opening into a hallway where the light has been burned out for the last twenty-five years.

Once in the narrow hallway, we turn right toward the break room. It's well lit with four round tables that don't match and about a dozen plastic chairs, left haphazardly wherever the last occupants had last sat. The walls are lined with vending machines selling soft drinks, coffee, candy and an over-used *Miss Pac-Man* game sits in the corner, quiet at the moment.

"Ya'll fire the maid?" laughs the Colonel, pointing at a garbage can in the corner that's way past needing to be emptied; one cup in and one falls out.

"Maid got caught up in the cutback, money was needed to upgrade the 'walk/don't walk' signs. Seems that when the walk sign was on, the man was white so all the signs had to be changed so the man was green."

"You got to be kidding! They changed all the walk lights because the guy was white?"

In the middle of telling him how they may have to change them again, this time because they are male and not unisex, Andy comes though the door carrying three cups of coffee. "Brought these from upstairs. The coffee in these machines sucks."

"Andy, this is Roger Nichols. He can help you with the pizza killing, if he will," I stand up and take a coffee from Andy.

The Colonel takes a cup from Andy saying, "Depends on what you need. I won't help you pin it on a homeless person."

"Roger, is it okay if I call you Roger?" asks Andy.

"Sure, that's my name. Conway calls me Colonel."

"Maybe I can call you Colonel?" Andy takes a sip of coffee, while hoping he might be making a friend

The Colonel glances over at me and then to Andy, "No, you cannot. I wish Conway wouldn't, but he didn't ask permission."

"Okay, then. Mr. Nichols, this is what I need from you. I need you to use your position at the mission to help me get some of the street people to talk to me," Andy says, sitting up straight in his chair, a practiced move by young detectives trying to look more experienced than their age would allow.

The Colonel and I both laugh. "Position at the mission? He's a wino!"

"What are you two up too?" Andy asks, obviously feeling like we were making a fool of him.

"If anyone can get you an audience with Maggie, he can."

"Maggie," the Colonel speaks up, "That woman comes in three forms; drunk, passed out, or crazy."

"I need to talk to her about the body she found in the salt pits."

"Over where the police drink beer and eat pizza?"

"Yeah, I need to ask her what she saw and if anyone was around when she was there."

"Well, first I need to have a truck driver arrested for taking money from Big Charlie saying it's for insurance."

"What's he talking about Conway?" Andy asks slowly, realizing that he's losing control of the conversation.

"There's a guy that lives in the wino camp down by the river and works for cash on the Hay Market," I start to explain. "He's a little slow, but never hurts anybody and is a hard worker. This truck driver tells him if he works on the truck, he has to pay ten dollars for insurance. The Colonel wants the driver to pay for mistreating him." I finish my story and my coffee, sitting the cup on the table.

"You help me Mr. Nichols, and I'll personally look into the truck driver," smiles Andy.

"All right, I can't get Conway to stop, so you might as well call me Colonel too."

"When can we get started with Maggie?" Andy asks eagerly, trying to move things along.

"Meet us at the liquor store on Market in about two hours. Change clothes and bring some money," I tell Andy.

"Why?"

The Colonel and I start for the door, but he stops to give Andy an ultimatum. "You think you're going to sit down with Maggie empty handed and ask questions? First, get out of that 'I'm better than you' coat and tie. Then, pick up a couple bottles of wine and a sack of dumpster burgers."

"What the hell is a dumpster burger?"

"Just change clothes, get a half dozen cheeseburgers at Mickey D's and meet us at the liquor store. Come alone. Never mind the wine, we'll get it. Just give me five dollars," I order him, turning with my hand out, palm up.

****

After getting two bottles of Night Train from the nice man behind the glass, the Colonel and I wait for Andy. An unmarked car pulls on the lot and we can see that there are two people in the car.

The Colonel looks at me with that 'what part of alone do you think this fool did not understand' expression. I know, because I was thinking the same thing.

The Captain gets out on the passenger side of the vehicle and starts walking toward my car. "Where the hell you think you're going?" I ask.

The Captain gives me a 'do you know who I am look' and says, "I'm going with you."

"No. You are absolutely not," answers the Colonel, calmly.

"I agree," I break in, for all the good it'll do.

Putting his hands on his hips, the Captain puffs up like a blowfish, "And why the hell not?"

Well, personally I've got three or four reasons; the deal was just Andy, added to the fact of course that ten-year-old, ill-fitting secondhand suit you're wearing and the fact that your tie has more stains than a painters drop cloth. But the real reason is that I don't like you and I don't trust you," the Colonel dismisses the Captain, turning his back to him.

"You can't talk to me like that. I'll lock your wino ass up," threatens the Captain, grabbing the Colonel by the arm.

"I can, I did, and I've been in jail before. I'll just be in jail again and you'll have an unsolved killing."

"What am I supposed to do if I don't go with you?" the Captain asks, letting go of the Colonel's arm and stepping back.

"I can help you with that, Captain. You can wait here, you can call a car to come and get you, or you can walk back to your office," I say, feeling full of myself.

Glancing over at Andy, I follow with, "Come on kid, bring your burgers. We're burning daylight."

Raising Andy, aka The Kid

After leaving the police car for the Captain, I promise I'll drop Andy back off at headquarters. The Colonel makes him sit in the backseat, holding the wine and burgers.

Once in the parking lot, we head down the path to the camp and Andy stops long enough on the way to point out where the body was found. Passing a four foot high concrete wall, I notice that the pit looks a lot different in daylight. There's a gravel driveway leading into the pit so the trucks can back in, but the lights on the towers that shine on the sand don't reach this area. This is where the cops walk down to piss.

Once we get to the camp, we see the fire going and Big Charlie and Maggie have emptied several bags of frozen vegetables into a big pot to make soup.

The Colonel yells out to let them know we're coming in and Maggie turns our way. Seeing the wine, her face lights up showing her missing teeth. Big Charlie tells us dinner will be ready as soon as Seven Eleven gets back from the mission with the paper bowls and crackers.

The Colonel turns to the kid, "I hope your wine goes with the vegetable soup."

"I don't think Night Train will go with anything but a brown paper bag," I laugh and then give the kid the same warning I had gotten, "It's your wine so you get the first drink."

"No, ladies first," Andy says in his best boy scout voice.

"Rules of the camp, Kid. You got the wine, you take the first drink," the Colonel says, pushing Maggie's hand away from the bottle.

"Listen to the Colonel, this is his home field and we're guests," I take the bottle from Andy and put it back in the bag.

The Colonel turns over a bucket and sits next to Maggie, who's eyes are locked in on the brown bag holding the Night Train. He maneuvers, so he's sitting between her and the bottle and asks, "Maggie, we need to know about the body you found over in the salt pit."

"What about the wine?" Maggie squirms, trying to look around the Colonel at the bag on the ground, fixated like a toddler on a new toy.

"First, you answer Conway and Andy's questions, then you can even have my part of the bottle," the Colonel leans over so Maggie has to look him in the eye.

From behind us, we hear a noise and all turn to find a man about forty-five dragging a refrigerator box. As proud as if he had purchased a mansion, he announces he's found a new home.

"This is Tony," Seven Eleven says from the unseen side of the refrigerator box.

Tony, standing with one hand on his box as if it would run away, sticks his other one out for Andy and me to shake. From his wornout work boots to his disheveled hair, he didn't feel homeless any longer. Spotting the brown bag on the ground and the soup on the fire, he smiles, "Looks like I got here in time for dinner."

"Got some paper bowls and crackers," Seven Eleven announces and dinner is served.

Maggie, still on her bucket, grumbles, "They won't let us drink if we don't tell them about the body over in the salt pit.

Seven Eleven pulls up an old cardboard box and sitting the crackers and bowls near the soup pot answers, "I was sure surprised when I found that man under all them pizza boxes."

Now, for the first time since he was told to listen to the Colonel, Andy's ears perk up. He's ready to sit Seven Eleven down and find out what he knows, but I put my hand on his shoulder urging him to sit still and let Seven Eleven tell his story.

"Me and Charlie saw the police over there when we was coming back from the liquor store. We had walked up to hang around the store, hoping to get someone to give us money for wine, but it was a slow night. So, just after dark we were coming down the trail when about four cop cars pulled in. I wanted to go over and see if they would give us some pizza and maybe a beer, but Charlie said no, that he didn't want to. If we was going over there, we could have gone when the blond in the yellow car and the three guys in the SUV was there. They looked like they had money and might give us some to move along," Seven Eleven continues.

"When did you see the yellow car and the SUV by the salt pit?" asks the Colonel.

"Before dark, when me and Charlie was walking up to the liquor store. I guess around four or five. You have better luck you know if you catch people on their way home from work."

Big Charlie, kneeling by the fire, dips out a bowl of soup and adds "Yeah, after we heard the police leave, we went over to see if they left any pizza or maybe part of a can of beer on the wall. It's hard to see in the pit after the sun goes down, so we took a flashlight with us."

"That's when we saw the body. Scared the shit out of me. I picked up a couple of boxes and there he was, just laying there looking up at the sky," Seven Eleven recalls, shaking his head.

"Ole scaredy cat here was gonna run, but I said let's check and see if he's got any money on him. He didn't have no watch or rings or wallet, so we got the left-over pizza and a half can of beer and came back to the camp." Big Charlie fills in the facts adding, "When we got here we told Maggie and I guess she told the lady at the mission."

One look at Andy and the Colonel and I know that if he doesn't get to ask some questions soon, he'll explode. But we need him to just be patient and the story will come out on its own. The Colonel is good at working Charlie and Seven Eleven for information.

"What were the blond and the three men doing?" explodes out of Andy's mouth.

Seven Eleven, having located the cheeseburgers, got the words out around half a burger. "They was talking and then one of the guys got in the car with the blond lady and the other men got in the van and drove up the truck road right past us real fast."

"Did you get a look at the people when they drove by?" Andy questions, scooting to the edge of the bucket he was seated on, causing it to tip up on the rim.

"The blond lady was in the passenger side and a big Mexican looking guy was driving, but there was so much dust we couldn't see in the van." Charlie answers.

"What about the wine?" whines Maggie.

Andy laughs so hard at the way Maggie jumped in the middle of the conversation checking on the wine that the bucket tips over and he lands flat on his butt. The bucket bounces into the three-legged chair leaning against the tree, sending the cat flying and vegetable soup spewing out of Tony's nose and all over his new home.

Helping Andy back to his feet, I hand the wine to Big Charlie. "I think I know who the blond is. We need to go to the photo lab for a mug shot."

"Charlie, would you or Seven Eleven be able to identify the woman if we showed you a picture?" asks Andy, still red faced after falling off the bucket.

Both men answer with a nod of their heads, wanting to be helpful. Maggie tries again to grab one of the wine bottles and, obviously unimpressed, the cat stares at us like we were big fat field mice.

This seems like a great time to leave.

Asking For Help

The walk back to the car is quiet, but the minute the doors all close the dam breaks and the questions come out of Andy's mouth rapid fire; "Did you hear about the beer? Who's the blond? Why do you think you know her? You think she killed that man?"

"He's talking so fast, if you stop him I think his tongue would come off the rollers," the Colonel rolls his eyes impatiently.

"I think he just realized he's jumped in the deep end of the pool and his only help is two old has-beens." I glance over my shoulder at Andy, who's leaning up between the seats.

"He's new at this undercover work, give the guy a break. He knows more about the killing now than the whole rest of the police department," says the Colonel, throwing a glance toward Andy.

Ready to chew a hole in the headrest, Andy is yelling in my ear, "So tell me how you know the blonde!"

"Okay, sit back and relax. If she's who I think she is, she's a hooker I locked up when I was working in the Organized Crime Unit. She was married to a Colombian who could easily be mistaken for a Mexican. So if it's who I think it is Kid, you're about to get a seat at the big table."

"What are you telling the kid?" The Colonel tries to catch up.

"I'm saying this could be a drug hit. The blonde's husband was a court interpreter for the feds until they found out he wasn't asking the questions they were asking or giving the answers they were supposed to be getting back. If it turns out to be him, you'll have the FBI, DEA, ICE and the whole alphabet soup group in your hair," I nod to the kid.

Knowing the kid was anxious about what he was getting into, the Colonel chuckles and says, "Not the FBI again. They almost got us killed when the First Lady was in town."

"That was the Secret Service, Colonel, not the FBI. Besides, this is the kid's deal," I remind him as we pull into a parking space outside the jail.

"Never went in this door. Got to come out once or twice," mused the Colonel.

"This is where the kid can get the picture of the blond. Her name is Mary Green, Kid. We'll wait here. Get enough pictures for a photo pack and three of Mary so they can sign the back if they pick her out," I remind him, turning in my seat so I can see Andy as he gets out of the car to head into the building.

"What are we going to do about the truck driver?" The Colonel settles in to wait for Andy to return.

"I have a plan. I think first we'll talk to the boss, then set the driver up so he can choose between paying back the money to Charlie or go to jail. Either way, he doesn't work at the Hay Market again. Will that make you happy?" I glance over at the Colonel.

"That'll make me happy," the Colonel responds with the hungry look of an animal on the track and then leans back with his eyes closed.

The kid returns to the car with a handful of mug shots, waving one of the pictures at me as he settles into the back seat. "Is this the lady you were talking about?"

"Yep, that's her."

"Well, let's go see if Charlie and Seven Eleven recognize her," Andy says, leaning forward in the seat with his head between mine and the Colonels.

But, I know there's work that needs to be done first. Parking a couple blocks over in front of police headquarters, I tell the kid to get out and get a copy of the file. "Some of the guys in your unit were at the salt pit the night the body was found. Let's find out who the players are before we make the circle any bigger."

I give him cell phone numbers to reach me or the Colonel and I get his, instructing him to only contact us on his cell phone and only when he's alone.

"What do I tell the Captain? You know he's going to question me about what we found."

"Tell him you talked to Maggie and she just heard about the body, but she never saw it, which is the truth," the Colonel says, being an authority on half-truths.

"What are you guys gonna do?"

"We're going to the Hay Market to talk to Mr. Silverman about the other problem," I respond, more for the benefit of the Colonel than the kid.

I'm From The Government And Nobody Is As Smart As Me

As we park near the Hay Market's back loading dock, I suggest to the Colonel that he let me do the talking, even though I know it's not likely to work out that way.

We locate Mr. Silverman right away who tells us to call him Paul, but his shoulders bent forward by age makes it difficult for me to call him anything but Mr. Silverman. He's wearing a pair of bib overalls over a flannel shirt that looks as if it has been on the dock as long as he has. He has to be about eighty years old and on that dock every day. I remember him from when my dad brought me to the market to get our Christmas tree when I was just a little kid, standing between him and my mom in the front seat.

After telling Paul about what's going on with the truck driver and Big Charlie, he's ready to fire the driver that day. But we ask him to wait until we have a chance to get the money back. He agrees to wait and promises to keep a better eye out.

Walking back to the car, the phone rings. I see Andy's number on caller ID, so I put the call on speaker so the Colonel can hear.

"What's going on, Kid?" I ask, as the Colonel moves closer to listen.

"The FBI is in the office wanting to talk to you guys," Andy whispers into the phone.

"How did they find out about us?" asks the Colonel.

"The Captain I guess."

"Are you by yourself?"

"No, the Captain and two FBI agents are standing around my desk like buzzards waiting for something to die."

"Tell those two school boys we appreciate the invitation, but no thanks. We're busy."

"They would like for you two to come to the office," Andy begs, wanting to get out of the hot seat with the captain.

"All right, tell them we'll meet 'em for lunch at my office and they're buying. Checks Bar, five o'clock. Back table."

"We'll be there." I can hear the relief in Andy's voice.

I look at the Colonel who's shaking his head in disbelief. It's obvious he has something to say. "Have you lost your mind? This is the FBI, you can't play with them like you did the boy in the coffee shop!"

****

Checks is a corner bar in the heart of Germantown. The lunch group is made up of CEOs, lawyers, police, firemen, factory workers and the unemployed. On the menu is bean soup, hot dogs, beer and brats, and during Lent it's standing room only for fish sandwiches. You order at the bar and pay, then have a seat and wait for the cook to step out of the kitchen and yell the order, so you can yell "Here" to indicate where you're sitting. The dinner crowd is not as busy, so we find a table in the corner facing the door.

"How'll we know when they get here?"

"We'll know because they'll stand out like a sore thumb. Besides, Andy'll be with them."

It's only a couple of minutes before the Captain, Andy and the two feds enter the room. The table we chose only has five chairs, which leaves the Captain with no place to sit.

After the introductions, I tell the agents what we'd like to eat and we get down to questions and answers.

From a chair pulled to the corner of the table the Captain says, "These two agents would appreciate your help in finding out who killed that man we found in the salt pit."

"First of all, these are not FBI agents. One of them is a U.S. Deputy Prosecutor that works with the DEA on drug cases, right?" I question the prosecutor, looking him right in the eyes.

"What the hell is a federal prosecutor doing working a street killing?" asks the Colonel with a bewildered expression on his face

"That's a good question and if they lie to us, I'll tell the story on the six o'clock news," I answer, never taking my eyes off the prosecutor.

"Why would we care if you tell the news or not, we're just trying to help," smirks the agent.

"Who was the guy that got himself killed?" I ask anyone who might answer.

"Jack Moore," answers the kid.

"Happy Jack Moore?" I ask Andy, taking a bite of my hot dog and a drink of coke.

"Yeah. Why? What difference does the name make?" pipes up the Captain.

"Let's start with the fact that these two are not here to help you do anything. So you can tell me and the Colonel the truth, or this meeting is over," I glare at him, sitting my coke can down hard on the tabletop for emphasis.

The prosecutor asks, "What are you talking about?"

"Happy Jack was a two-bit thug and snitched to stay out of jail. You were using him on a drug deal, it got him killed and now you're trying to clean up the mess before Washington finds out. Because, if they do you'll be prosecuting salmon poachers in Alaska and your buddy will be investigating missing footlockers on some out of the way army post. Now, tell me I'm wrong." I wait for an answer while I finish my hotdog.

The Feds looked at one another and then back at the Colonel and me. From the puzzled look on their faces, I realize that telling the truth might take some thought for these two, and I feel the need to give them some space.

The whole place is quiet and down to a few patrons. A bookie is sitting on a stool at the end of the bar taking bets from a couple of neighborhood gamblers. The house phone is sitting in front of him, so he can take bets from the folks who can't get there. A middle-aged couple at a table are finishing up their bean soup and holding hands before going home to their respective husband and wife. Two men, dressed as if they just got off work at the garage across the street, are standing in the middle of the room watching the news and cussing the government. A bar is definitely a poor man's university.

I pick up my empty coke can and motion to the Colonel by tilting my head in the direction of the bar, "How about another round? I'll buy."

The kid jumps to his feet saying, "Me too, you guys."

We glance at the feds still sitting at the table, then the three of us walk to the bar where the bartender reluctantly pulls himself away from the TV to take our order. The Captain finally catches on that the feds need alone time and joins us at the bar.

Over my shoulder, I can see the two at the table in deep discussion. After giving them a few minutes alone, I grab hot dogs and cokes and we return to the table. "Got you guys cokes and dogs too," says the kid, unloading everything onto the table.

"Thanks, Detective. You're right, Conway. But we'll need your help. Will you work with us?" asks the prosecutor with a puppy dog look on his face.

Knowing he's playing to my ego, I sit back in my chair playing his game. "You two going to treat the kid like he's an equal? Because that's who I'm gonna work with," I tell them with the same tone I use when questioning a suspect, the ones I know I have, but they haven't figured it out yet.

The prosecutor, being the spokesperson for the team answers, "We'll tell you what we can."

"Not good enough, all or nothing. We'll be seeing you guys, thanks for dinner." I stand so they have to look up at me.

"Wait, we'll tell you what we know and we'll keep the kid in the loop," the prosecutor relents.

"Okay, we'll see you guys in the morning. Get the file together and I'll call you where to meet us. You agree that the circle for right now will be you two, the kid and only the kid, the Colonel and me?"

I finish my second hot dog, wiping the mustard from my mouth with the back of my hand and start for the door where the Colonel is waiting. It's obvious from his actions he's uncomfortable around cops.

The Colonel's First Stake-Out

The next morning I turn into the driveway of the farm just as the sun is starting to shine though the old oak tree and light up the red roofs of the barns. Young horses in the front field race the car up to the house from their side of the fence.

Pulling up, I find the Colonel sitting on the front steps with a cup of coffee. After sitting his cup down next to a clay pot filled with pink and dark purple petunias, he walks over to the car and climbs in. Looking down at the two cups in the console, he asks, "Which one is mine? Don't want to catch anything you might have."

"Catch my germs? You're the one who eats out of the dumpster. Yours is the one in the back," I finally say, pulling out onto the paved road.

****

It's daylight when we pull into the gravel lot of the Hay Market and park where we can see the loading dock. Several farm trucks have already backed in, waiting for the markets to open. We watch as some restaurants in the area stop by to pick some of the corn and tomatoes right off the back of the trucks. As a uniformed officer on his walking beat through the neighborhood passes though the lot, one of the drivers calls him by name and throws him an apple. The officer smiles, waves and keeps walking.

Settling in to wait for Charlie and the driver, I lean back in my seat. "I've got a question for you Colonel, and I think we've been through enough that I can ask it. I've noticed that you're black as coal and the rest of your family looks like snowflakes."

He reaches into the bag sitting next to the coffee for some creamer, never taking his eyes off the dock.

"You noticed? What was it, my curly hair?"

"How did that happen?"

"There wasn't much chance of my going to college; no money, no job and the Army looked like a way out of the life I hated, so I joined up. After boot camp, I made my way to war. No parties and no friends at the bus station, just a cold rainy morning in August."

The Colonel stops to take a drink of hot coffee and we both sit quiet for a few minutes. He's wearing that 'hundred yard stare' on his face again as he looks out the windshield and I'm left wishing I had the question back.

Then, without the expression on his face changing or breaking his stare, the Colonel begins again, "That's when I met Joe. I was on a two man listening post on Hill 661. When the copters started in, they were coming in on the wrong side of the little valley which was not something new, because they landed about half the time in the wrong spot. It was raining as I watched the door on the back open and dump its contents onto the muddy ground. Once on the ground, it looked like someone had emptied a sack of cats when they ran in all directions."

Working hard to tie this story to the question of why he was black and the rest of the family was white, I just listened and hoped for the best.

After taking a breath and gulping down his coffee, the Colonel continued his story. "That's when Joe fell into the hole I was in. The whole world out there and this waste of skin had to find me trying to hide from him. Look, there's the truck."

Reaching over to get a hold on the Colonel before he can get out, I say, "Sit here so we can see what happens. We want to get it right the first time, so we need to watch what the driver does when Charlie gets here. Now, back to the story."

"What are we watching for, so I know when I see it?"

"I want to see when and how the money changes hands so we'll know when and how to catch the truck driver. Now, what happened once you and Joe were in the same foxhole?"

I'm more into the Colonel's story than I am into keeping an eye on the driver.

"Hey, there's Charlie," the Colonel leans forward as if those few inches would give him a better view.

Big Charlie walked straight up to Mr. Silverman, who gave him some money. Then, Charlie walked to the truck and the driver held out his hand for his insurance money.

"Can we lock him up now?" the Colonel asks, scrambling to get out of the car.

"No, now we call the kid and have him call the feds to meet us."

I back up to pull out of the lot and call the kid's cell phone, putting it on speaker. "Call the feds and have them meet you at the liquor store on Market. Tell them to remember to bring the file."

"You guys gonna be there?"

"No, but we'll be close. After you meet them, let them follow you to the crime scene. I don't trust them to come alone, so we'll make sure no one follows", I say looking the Colonel in the eye.

The FBI Don't Change Their Spots

We park our car on Seventh Street north of Broadway where the feds keep their cars. This gives us a good view of the parking garage exit. We're not there long enough to get the Colonel to pickup on his story, because in a couple minutes the prosecutor and the agent who appears to be his sidekick come out. They turned their dark green mid-size Chevy north on Seventh and are followed by a second mid-size light blue Chevy with two other agents. We follow them down Seventh Street to Market and then east to the liquor store. The traffic is just right for tailing someone; not so heavy you might lose them, but not so thin that you might be spotted.

The prosecutor and the agent pull their car up next to the kid's car. The other car comes to a stop about a half a block away and parks. We drive past and pull in a lot across the street, so we can see all three cars. I have to guess, after some small talk, the kid asks about the file because the prosecutor holds up a file jacket and the kid nods. The kid talks for a minute more and drives off,

114

followed by the prosecutor, followed by the second car, followed by us.

"We need a parade permit?" asks the Colonel in his own personal sarcastic tone.

The kid and the prosecutor turn into the limestone driveway leading to the salt pit where Happy Jack's body was found. As the dust from the tires block the view, the other car stops on the street, just past the entrance so it can't be seen from the lot. We drive into the lot and up to the prosecutor's car, close enough so that the limestone dust from our tires now covers their immaculate dark blue suits.

Once the air clears and we get the smiles off our faces, the Colonel turns to me, "The two men in the car parked on the street are the same two guys who were in the bar last night at the dinner meeting."

"Don't say anything. It looks like the feds are not going to play by the rules, so go along with what I say." Winking, I climb out of the car.

After waiting for both federal clowns to stop brushing the dirt off their suit and looking at us like they know we did it on purpose, I offer my hand to the agent. Looking him in the eye, I ask, "You guys bring the files?"

"Sure," answers the prosecutor, holding up the file while still brushing his hand over his suit..

"Tell us what you know and if we know anything different, we'll fill you in," pipes up the agent.

"Got a better idea. Let's have a look at the file and then we'll fill you guys in. After all, you've been dealing with this a lot longer than us," I remind them, reaching for the folder.

After checking the file and seeing that it's redacted to past useful I remark, "This is not a clean file, boys. In fact, this one page has everything blacked out but the page number. That leads me to believe you don't want to play nice with others. So, on your way out don't forget the two other suits on the road." I can feel the 'lets be friends' tone leaving my voice.

"There are no agents on the road, you're being paranoid," growls the agent, still dusting his suit and wanting to be a player at a game where he's riding the bench.

"Okay, one more chance. We talked to the street people who live over by the river. They said a guy named Big Charlie works for a guy at the Hay Market unloading the trucks. We know that the truck driver gets ten dollars from Big Charlie everyday so we have to assume he's selling Charlie dope. I think Happy Jack found out the driver was moving drugs on the farm truck and was going to tell if he didn't give him a cut."

I glance over at the Colonel, reminding him to just go along.

"So you think the driver killed Happy Jack?" asks the prosecutor.

"It would be on the way back to the truck farm," the Colonel waves his hand across the view of the sandlot and cuts off the prosecutor's question.

"We'll set up a time when you and your lapdog can meet us and then we'll see if we can get the folks down by river to talk to you. They have as high opinion of the FBI as I do," I say nonchalantly, fiddling with the wrapper on a cherry *Dumb Dumb* sucker I got from Andy.

Without waiting for an answer from Frick and Frack, I add, "Come alone. If you get caught playing games again, we're done," knowing I was poking a verbal stick at the agent who's blood pressure was causing his face to become bright red.

"You don't give us orders, who do you think you are?" the agent says, exploding. Not being able to control himself any longer, he assumes a defensive stance.

"I'm the guy who was doing this job when you two still believed in Santa Claus and the Easter Bunny. And the guy you need to get the street people to talk to you and help you clear up this mess before it gets out. But if you don't want our help, I understand," I smile, talking around the sucker stick in the corner of my mouth.

Taking out my cell phone, I dial my home number, knowing no one is there. I look at the prosecutor and say into the phone, "News desk please. Yeah, is Bob Dish in? Well, tell him to call me. I have news about the body the police found on River Road. Retired Detective Conway. Yeah, this number will be fine."

"Wait, you're right. We can use your help. But the agent is also right, we can get along without you, you won't be making the rules," the prosecutor said, reaching for the file.

Handing the file to him I smile saying, "Come on, Colonel. We'll take Andy to lunch, dumpster burgers all around."

The two feds get in their car, use their two-way radio and a light blue mid-sized Chevy turns in and follows the prosecutor to an area as far away as they can get. The Colonel, with a smile reaching from ear to ear, waves at the two agents who had been waiting on the road as they exited the car.

"What are we gonna do now?" Andy asks, jumping up and down with excitement from putting the FBI in their place.

"You're going to show the photo pack to Big Charlie and Seven Eleven and if they pick out our girl, then we'll need to meet with the vice unit," I say watching as the Feds meet up. I didn't need to hear what was being said, but I could see the prosecutor's hands and if he was not Italian or Irish, he was not happy. When the two agents who had just arrived from the road wave back at the Colonel, the prosecutor angrily throws the file in the car. Then, after a short meeting, rocks and dust fill the air as the two cars leave the lot like they had some place important to be.

Back in the car, the Colonel and I start for the farm and lunch when the Colonel asks, "What's going to happen when the FBI talks to the group at the camp?"

"Well, first the crew at the river won't tell them anything because they don't know anything," I answer, turning onto River Road from the lot and heading for the expressway and the Colonel's house.

"The feds think the driver is the answer to their trouble and they'll go after him so they can make the arrest, control the case and protect their reputation. That'll serve the purpose we want by getting the driver messed with, as only the feds can do. It keeps them out of the way in this case."

"How long you think it'll take for them to figure out you lied to them?" worries the Colonel, not wanting the FBI after him.

"I didn't lie. Charlie does work for the truck driver on the Hay Market, right? We did talk to the people down by the river and they are street people, right? This is on the way to the truck farm and the driver gets ten dollars from Charlie every day, right? So, what's the lie?"

"You said you believed that the truck driver killed Happy Jack," the Colonel said, trying to point out the untruths.

"I never said I believe the truck driver killed Happy Jack. As to what the feds heard, who knows? Now, how about lunch?" I ask.

"Sis said she would fix lunch when I called her from the lot. Sandwiches okay?" asks the Colonel.

"That'd be great. She making them or fishing them out of the trash?"

"Well, aren't you the comedian?"

"Will you finish the story about the hill?" I ask, not having any plans for the rest of the day.

Still looking out the window as the faraway look returns to his eyes, the Colonel answers quietly, "We'll see."

Lunch On The Farm

The ride to the farm from River Road is about twenty minutes, most of which is in silence. The Colonel stares out the window, obviously thinking about the past.

Once back in the 'here and now', he asks what I thought the FBI would do next.

"I think they'll send a team to watch the driver and work a couple of undercover agents in to try to buy some drugs from him. They'll try to get them to move into the camp and get the street people to talk to them," I answer, never taking my eyes off the road.

"The truck driver don't sell dope, the street people know nothing and they sure don't take in strangers. Besides, what are they going to learn from following the guy back and forth from the farm?" the Colonel asks, still staring out the window.

"First, we told the feds what we knew and they're the ones that jumped to a conclusion," I reply.

"They didn't jump to a conclusion, they were pushed. You're going to get us arrested by the feds."

Turning into the long driveway leading up to the house, the mood of the Colonel changes, a smile crosses his face and a light glows in his eyes. We see his sister sitting in a porch swing hanging from two white chains at the far end of the front porch. Dressed in a red tee shirt and jeans, she's pushing the swing gently back and forth with one bare foot as she sips a glass of sweet tea. It's like looking at a scene from a southern movie.

As the car rolls to a stop, she starts down the steps complaining, "Where have you two been, anyway? I've had lunch ready for over an hour."

The Colonel turns facing me and places both hands on top of the car, "You remember my sister, Deana, from the hospital?

"Nice seeing you again, young lady," I nod at Deana.

"Is chow something we can carry down by the lake?"

"Clubs on toast and potato salad. Why the picnic by the lake?" Deana asks, hands on her hips and feet apart like she was ready to fight.

"I'm hoping I get to hear the story about what happened in Nam on the hill," I insert, as excited as a kid leaving school on a sunny day.

Deana's mood lightens, and she invites herself to lunch saying, "I want to hear about that too. That's where Roger and my brother Joe met."

"Lunch, please," the Colonel interrupts.

Deana hurriedly puts the food into a picnic basket. Handing her brother a large pitcher of sweet tea, she leads the way down a brick walk lined with rose bushes and leading the way to a large white gazebo, like you might picture in a park setting. After setting the pitcher in the middle of a round table, the Colonel settles himself into a comfortable-looking wicker chair. Deana sets glasses, napkins and plates holding a club sandwich and potato salad on the table at each place. I follow pouring the tea and join Deana on one side of the table facing the Colonel.

"Well?" Taking a bite of salad, Deana looks her brother in the eye.

The Colonel sighs, looks down at his plate and then up at Deana. "The first time I saw Joe he was rolling down a muddy hill. Myself and another soldier had just got to our listening post when the copters came in on the wrong side of the hill. The VC opened fire and a round tearing though the trees hit my partner in the chest. He was dead before he hit the ground." Taking a deep breath, the Colonel wipes a tear from his eye and continues, "I settled into a hole under the jungle so thick it blocked out the sunlight, waiting for a chance to carry my partner back to the base camp, when this wet-behind-the-ears boot falls in the hole on top of me. A cocky white boy who looked down on anyone who didn't belong to the country club."

Deana getting that 'hands on hips' look on her face says, "That was my brother."

"That's right. I expected him to have me get his bags and maybe a drink from the bar. He endeared himself to me once he realized I was black by referring to me as boy."

The story stops as a group of noisy geese land on the lake and I ask, "What was wrong with that?"

Deana chokes on a bite of her sandwich and the Colonel shakes his head and grins, calling me a redneck honky.

Taking a drink of tea, he returns to the story. "I see he's a boot and scared, so I introduce myself as Roger and ask his name. He tells me his name is Joe, that he hurt his knee when he fell and he wasn't sure he could walk. I told him I couldn't see in the dark, and with all the mud I couldn't tell if he was bleeding. When I reached in my pack and pulled out an apple and a K-bar fighting knife to cut it in half, Joe looked at me and I laughed, 'Does a black man with a knife scare you?' That's when we both knew we'd be friends." Deana and the Colonel both had tears running down their faces, remembering Joe.

Suddenly, we hear what sounded like a busload of rowdy kids coming down the path behind us. We turn to see the two little girls running down the hill yelling, "Uncle Roger, Uncle Roger!" as loud as they can. Laughing, Deana jumps up remembering she had agreed to watch the girls. Heading them off about halfway up the trail, she leaves the Colonel and myself to clean up.

Having not yet learned how he got to be part of the family, I ask a question hoping for an answer. "A lot of guys become friends in Nam and don't end up in a family like you did."

"You're about the nosiest white boy I think I ever met, but I guess that's why you were a good detective," said the Colonel putting the last of the dishes in the basket.

"Joe and I talked though the night. I told him I was from a poor family. My dad worked on a farm and he and Mom didn't have money for me to go to college, so I went into the Army hoping that my two sisters could go. Joe said he'd ask his dad if he could find a place in the business for my dad, but I warned him that Dad can't know, he'd see it as charity and he'd never take a handout."

"Joe promised me it wouldn't be charity. His daddy needed a good man to run the farm and it would come with an apartment. As the sun started up, I could see four VC had stopped for breakfast in the clearing about a hundred yards away. An army platoon came over the ridge and the VC ran right at us. Joe's knee had swollen and he couldn't get on his feet so I jumped up and yelled so they'd turn and follow me away from him. The soldiers got two, I got one, and the other one disappeared into the jungle. We got Joe ready and put him on a copter to be air-lifted out. That was the last time I saw or heard from him until I was back in the states. I did get a letter from my pop who wrote me that a man had offered him a job running a farm near Louisville and there was a place for him, Mom, and the two girls to live right on the farm. When I got back, Joe was already here. He told me his daddy and mine got along great and that Pop rode around on a golf cart all day and ran the place like it was his own. Joe had told his dad how I had saved his bacon on the hill. After my dad and mom both passed and the girls were off to college, his dad tried to adopt me but because of my age that was impossible. So he had me put in his will and from then on I was one of the family."

Time To Solve A Murder

All the way home I thought about what the Colonel said happened on the hill and how he'd become a member of the family. That still didn't answer the question as to why he had left all that to live on the street.

I was going over the story in my head for the twentieth time when the phone rang and the sound brings me back to the present. Seeing it's the kid, I check the time. Six-thirty. Why is he still working?.

"Hello, Kid."

"Big Charlie and Seven Eleven both picked out Mary's picture. I called vice and talked to Detective Thomas.

He's going to meet us tomorrow at the Brass Rail around lunchtime," the kid says, so wired up I know there'll be no sleep for him tonight.

"Where did you see Charlie and Seven Eleven?" I ask, giving the kid a chance to tell his story. I can hear the air he's sucking in, so that once he starts his story, he'll have that out of the way,

"I stopped by the liquor store on Market and got two bottles of *Night Train*, just like you guys would do. When I got to the camp, Maggie was sitting on her bucket by the fire making something she calls potato soup, Charlie was petting the cat and Seven Eleven was getting some firewood. Maggie smiled so big when she saw the wine, I could count all five of her teeth! I told them I had some business to do first. Needless to say that wasn't what Maggie wanted to hear."

"Sounds like our little boy is growing up."

"It felt good to sit'em down and have each one look at the photos and then sign the back. I taped the photo packs closed and put them along with an investigation letter in the file. When I called vice and talked to Thomas, I didn't tell him anything except I needed his help on a case. Did I do all right?" the kid asks, looking for my approval.

"You done good boy, you done good. See you at the Brass Rail around twelve-thirty."

"See you tomorrow," he's almost yelling from excitement.

I called the Colonel to let him know about tomorrow and what time I'll be picking him up, then I start for home to try to get some rest. I suspect it may be a long day tomorrow and I'm almost as excited as the kid.

****

The next morning starts off as usual. After Maureen's off to work, I make the bed, clean up last night's dishes and spend an hour at the gym. After a shower, I start on the half hour drive to the Colonel's house. The sky is bright blue, the sun is shining and I'm *back in the game*.

The Colonel is waiting on the porch steps. For a guy who doesn't help the police, he sure is anxious to get started. Standing on the third step from the top, he covers them in one stride. After a few more long strides to the car, the Colonel is in his seat and buckled up before I'm even sure the car has stopped.

"Good morning, you sure are in a good mood," I say, greeting the Colonel with a cup of coffee.

"Yesterday's lunch was great. Sis and I talked for a long time after the girls went to sleep. Joe has been the elephant in the room since he was killed," the Colonel says, looking out the windshield as if he could see the past. "What I told you back in the beginning was only partly true. I told you what would get me lunch. A lot of people will buy you something to eat or give you money for a sad story about the war. I figured you to be a veteran and too smart to buy just any bullshit story, so I gave you something with a little truth in it."

"I've been around the streets and the courts long enough to know that some victims of the war were never in the military and some drunks who blame their drinking on the war would have been drunks anyway," I respond, turning to glance over at the Colonel as we locate a parking spot near the Brass Rail Bar.

Just inside the door we notice the lights are just bright enough for you not to fall over a chair or table and just enough to allow us to see that the place is about half full. The bar starts just inside on the right and runs halfway down the long narrow room where it turns into a steam table for lunch. The left side of the room is all tables.

The kid and Detective Wayne Thomas are already at a table with a lunch plate. Although the bar isn't known for great food, it's still a good hangout for professional people. Two men sitting at the bar are settling up horse bets from yesterday as they study a racing form and a young man, maybe thirty, is in the back corner table with a box of tape players, watches and tools. This is known for being a place that you can get what you want, no questions asked.

After filling our plates, we walk over to their table and Wayne and the kid stands. As Andy starts to introduce us, Wayne stops him saying, "I know who this guy is. They still tell stories about him and his partner, Don, in the academy. Just call me Wayne, these people don't know I'm the police and I do business with some of them from time to time, if you know what I mean. I told a guy in here awhile back that my lawnmower broke and I was going to run by Sears to get one. About an hour later, he dropped off a nice mower, still warm, with the gas already in it. Now, what can we do for you guys?"

"You know a lady named Mary Green?" I asked.

"Everybody who works hookers or dopers knows Mary, but because of the dude she's married to, the feds always want a favor when we arrest her," Wayne answers, biting his lip in frustration.

"We need your help because we think she was around when Happy Jack got his," I said, pleased we had someone willing to help deal with the feds.

"I'm in, whatever you need. But I'm telling you, the feds are gonna steal your case and then dismiss it," Wayne says, speaking from experience..

"Well, for one thing they're busy chasing their tail and they can't afford to step in front of this one because they're responsible for the screw up that got Happy Jack killed in the first place. Pass the ketchup, this food is really bad. We need to get Mary out on a call, catch her and give her a chance to tell us what she knows about the killing and the drug operation," I tell him, covering my whole plate of food with ketchup.

"This is like eating at the mission if I could only get one of these folks to pray for my soul until the food gets cold and the ice in the drink melts," the Colonel contributes to the conversation.

Andy laughs, "The food here came cold and there wasn't that much ice in the drinks to start with."

"If we live though this lunch, I'll get a room at the Holiday Inn and we'll set it up for tonight. I'll get the rest of my team to help, they'll enjoy sticking it to the FBI," Wayne grins, while making quick notes on a napkin.

"Meet you on the parking lot at Wayside. Six o'clock should be early enough that she won't already be on a call and make us wait. We can wire the room and put the Colonel in there, I'm sure she won't know him," I say, smiling at the puzzled look that came over the Colonels face.

"Works for me," says Wayne, finishing his coke and starting for the door. The rest of us get up to leave as the Colonel takes a last bite of his lunch. Andy and I make a sour face and keep walking. Outside, the kid turns to the right as we head to our car on the left and I tell the him that we'll see him tonight.

Looking For Answers

The food at the Brass Rail was terrible, I'm still hungry and we have about three hours before we meet the kid and Thomas.

"Where you want to go eat?" I ask, almost before the car door closes.

"The food wasn't that bad. I'm not really hungry, but I will take a muffin and a cup of coffee. Got a hundred questions about tonight," the Colonel says in a worried voice.

"Let's go to the coffee shop then. We can go across the street to the liar's bench, I got a question or two myself."

"About Joe getting killed, I bet. You're driving," the Colonel said, but not sad like before.

The coffee shop and bench being just half a mile down Jefferson Street, and after hitting all green lights, we look for a parking space alongside the hotel on Third Street within minutes of leaving the Brass Rail.

As we get out of the car, what appears to be a fugitive from a Goodwill bag asks the Colonel if he had change to spare. The Colonel smiles, handing this follow traveler a couple of bucks saying, "Time to pay it forward I guess."

The coffee shop has more people in it than the Brass Rail did for lunch and we find ourselves in line behind two visitors to our fair city dressed to impress in black pantsuits, white blouses and large stone necklaces. Sitting at an open table near the cash register, they begin voicing loud complaints about the number of homeless people hanging out in front of the hotel looking for a handout. As they aimed their complaints at two police officers sitting at a table nearby, the officers finish their coffee and stand. We watch as one officer turns to the lady doing most of the talking and says in a most southern gentlemanly manner, "You ladies can have our table. It has a great view of the street and the front of the hotel."

Stifling a laugh, I order a sandwich, a muffin for the Colonel and two large coffees. Crossing the street to the liar's bench at the bus stop, we can see the ladies at the window table, pointing out to each other and anyone that can hear about the homeless.

As we take a seat on the bench, I realize that it seems like only yesterday I met the Colonel, but so far we've been in a shoot-out and a robbery, met the First Lady and stole breakfast from the Days Inn.

Taking a bite out of my sandwich, I watch the Colonel fighting the heat-wrapped packaging on his muffin. "Just not a dumpster burger is it?"

"No, it ain't, but maybe we can get a sackful for the team tonight. The kid looked like he could use a burger," answers the Colonel. "If you're ready for why I ended up on the street, I can't think of a better place to tell the story than right here on the bench."

"I'm ready if you are, Colonel."

"Well, I'd just got back to the world and Joe had gotten home a month before me. For the first week or two, we would sit by the lake, mostly telling funny stories about the military and taking about four hot showers a day. You know how good a hot shower feels when you first get home?"

After another sip of coffee and finishing off the last bite of his muffin, he continues, "But before long, both of our dad's had a 'come to Jesus' with us at the picnic table. Joe's dad did most of the talking, but we knew the two dads had talked beforehand. His dad told us it was time to go to work, and he had a deal for us if we wanted it. He said he'd pay for us to go to the community college and for our books, but we had to work on the farm for my dad and use our VA money and what he paid us for clothes, gas and walking around money. Joe wanted to go back to the same university he had flunked out of before going in the service. But, both dads agreed that wasn't gonna happen, so we took the deal."

The Colonel finishes off his coffee and starts again; he is so ready to get this off his chest. "The community college wasn't so bad. There was a group of veterans who hung together, not wanting to deal with the just out of high schoolers who all had dreams to be doctors or lawyers and make lots of money. Most of the kids there still lived at home and the ink was still wet on their high school diplomas, but they used all of their worldly knowledge to call us baby killers, burn the flag and have sit-ins against the war. The black-and-white issue wasn't as bad for me because most of the veterans sat together; black, white, Indian, two Mexicans and even a woman that you could not tell from one of the guys in her camo, but was a fox in a dress. Most of the kids there were about half scared of us and I believe some of the teachers were too. Sometimes, one of the boys wanting to show off would catch one of the vets and confront him about the war. Most of the time, the vet would just walk away. The kid would feel like a big man on campus and the vet would feel he had saved the kid an ass-whopping."

"The trouble came away from school when we were out walking around shopping and ran into some kids from the Country Club, dressed in their penny loafers with no socks, dockers and button-down dress shirts. They were drunk and looking for a fight when they spotted us."

The big mouth in the group started with "Hey, Joe you got your pet out for a walk?"

"What did you say punk?" Joe said, puffing up.

"I said you got your monkey out for a walk?" Being full of liquid courage, the little puke pointed a finger at me.

Getting nose to nose with him, Joe says, "I think you owe my friend an apology."

"I ain't apologizing to that coon," Big Mouth said, looking back and forth to his friends for support.

Joe hit him right in the nose before Moses got the news. There was blood, snot, and sweat everywhere. The other two stepped back, not having the stomach for a fight now that it was two on two. They weren't that drunk.

I got Joe by the arm and turned him in one direction and they picked up the bully with the bloody nose and carried him off in another direction. Thinking it was over, we started for the car. As we crossed the parking lot, Big Mouth and his friends stepped out from behind a van. It was shaping up to be round two.

Looking over his shoulder, Joe told them, "You guys go on now. It's over."

"Not by a long shot," the hooligan snarled, and pulled a gun from under his blood-stained shirt.

"He quickly fired four shots, sending us ducking between the cars for cover. I was hit one time in the shoulder and it burned like hell, but being the target I felt lucky. As I watched them run away, I started looking for Joe. He was hit once in the chest and once in the stomach. I called 911 and held him as he died in my arms. After that, I was worried that the family thought I was at fault. Joe's dad still called me son and paid for my school, but I would sit in the basement and drink. When my mom died, I was too drunk to go. That's when my dad came home from the funeral and said I had to straighten up or get out. I left and never looked back. Sold my car for money and got a job or two, but drinking still helped me forget. That's not true, I would get drunk, then cry myself to sleep in some alley. The next day would be like the day before. I got hurt real bad when I got hit by a bus. The family came to the VA and took me home, but when the pain killers ran out, I started drinking again and Joe's dad said I couldn't be around the girls. So I went to the only place I knew, the street. Now, there's the truth. You still want to be around me?"

"Colonel, you're one of the best men I know. Children know too and those two little girls love you," I say finishing my coffee. "Now, let's go see the kid."

Hooker Hunting

The Colonel's been awfully quiet since we got back in the car to go meet the group to catch Mary. Finally, in a little boy voice he asks, "You guys aren't going to embarrass me, are you?"

"You walked around town wearing a pair of dirty brown suit pants that's way too big, held up by a wide powder blue necktie with a hula girl on it. What could we possibly do that would be more embarrassing than that?" I ask, laughing at the picture in my mind.

"I was drunk most of the time. I just want to know what's gonna happen tonight," he answers, still worried about what we would ask him to do.

"You'll check in the hotel and go to your room. The team will have it wired because you aren't police and if it goes to trial, we'll have to back up your word. Then, you'll make the call. Thomas has the number and will tell you what to say. All the props you'll need will be in the room. Then, you just have to wait for Mary."

I'm not sure that the Colonel believes me as we pull onto the shelter's parking lot and find Detective Thomas, the kid and four other members of the team already there. Thomas steps up to the car and, leaning in the window on the Colonel's side asks, "You ready, Colonel?"

"I hope I don't let you down," the Colonel says, still not sounding sure about what's getting ready to go down.

"Room 624 has already been wired. You'll just need to check in at the desk. Your cover story is that your house is being painted, and the smell gives you a headache. We don't trust everyone who works here," Thomas steps back, letting the Colonel exit the car.

Once I reached the other side of the car, I hear Thomas say, "We get a key from the manager we've worked with before and the owner says we can trust him. The owner wants to keep the call girls out of his hotel and appreciates our help, so when we need a room for a detail he sees that we have what we need. We go into the room before our undercover checks in and the manager makes sure we get that room. Some of the desk clerks and bell boys pick up good money watching for the police. Once the call is made from the room to the service, the girl will call back to the hotel and check with someone they give some money to, making sure the guy is not the police."

"Why would they help them, knowing that the hotel wants the service out?" asks the Colonel.

"Colonel, we have people who work for the police department, but also work with the call girl service by telling them when the team is out working and where. So, like tonight, we don't turn in a line-up so the radio room doesn't know we're out. That's also why, in this case, we have to be really careful," Thomas says shaking his head.

"It's a game, Colonel. Some we win and some we lose. You ready to make the call?" I ask, looking from the Colonel to Thomas. I'm so ready to get 'back in the game'.

"You check in and go to your room. From there, you make the call and tell the person that answers the phone that a friend gave you the number and said to ask for Wanda. Tell them your friend said she was a blond, about twenty-five. She'll ask you if you're going to use a credit card or cash. Tell her cash. Once you have a time she's going to arrive, order something from room service, run some water in the shower and dampen a towel and throw it on the floor. Then wet down a wash cloth and leave it in the shower. Take off your shoes and socks, lay on the bed and move the pillows around like you've been napping, and pull your shirttail out. Open the suitcase and pull something part of the way out so it looks like you were getting things out, then close the top down." Thomas laid out the way to set the scene.

"That's a lot to do just to catch one hooker. They don't do this on TV," the Colonel grumbles, but starts to get into his role.

Thomas looks at him, then me and smiles, saying, "On TV, the hookers are high school dropouts, dopers, and young runaways. This lady has a bachelors degree in art and was trained by a lady who earned her masters degree in social services, couldn't find a job in her field, started this business and was good enough that she walked on federal charges by the FBI." He continues, "This hooker will check the room and if she thinks you're a cop, she'll walk out. They're making five hundred to a thousand dollars a night, more when a convention is in town or during Derby week. A radio in the bottom of the suitcase will allow us to hear what's going on in the room. You got questions?"

"Do I get a gun?"

"No!", Thomas and I answer at the same time.

"Well, what do I use if there's trouble?"

"Your wit," I answer.

"You ready? We're burning daylight," Thomas says.

The Colonel nodded, got out of the car and headed for the hotel entrance to check in. The kid and I sit with Thomas in his unmarked car in the front of the hotel. There's one of his team on every entry door because the girls want to get in and out without passing the front desk.

Fifteen minutes later we hear the Colonel open the latch on the suitcase, move clothes around and close it again. We can now hear him make the call from the bedside phone, "Hello, is this Wanda? Yeah. A friend gave me this number and said to ask for Wanda. His name is Joe. Cash. I'm at the Holiday Inn on Jefferson Street, Room 624. Seven-thirty would be great, tell Wanda I'll be waiting. Yes, two hundred dollars cash."

Thomas turned in the seat, "This guy is a natural. Now we wait."

The Colonel is now running water in the shower, ordering dinner and moving around in the room. The kid, fidgeting, is mumbling about wishing something would happen.

"Patience, Kid. Don't they teach that in the academy?"

"No, just crossing the T's and dotting the I's. Most of the instructors couldn't carry water to a real policeman," Thomas says over his shoulder. "I remember the old guy who trained me had three rules. One you go home, two your partner goes home, and three help some of the people who need it. But always rule one and two first."

"Those are the rules I learned," I lean back in my seat to concentrate on the radio and watch the comings and goings in the parking lot.

We hear a knock on the hotel door and we all sit up to listen. "Room service," a man's voice yells.

We hear the door open and then the Colonel's voice, "Sit it here and this is for you."

Seconds later we hear a woman's voice say, "Are you Roger?"

"You must be Wanda."

Gotcha

Everyone is on the edge of their seats, trying to get close to the wire receiver, not wanting to miss a word of what's said in the room. One of the team members reports that the driver went up with Mary. Thomas tells the team to get inside the hotel and stay out of sight, in case this is a rip-off.

"If he's just taking her to the room and getting the money, let him get back to the car, but don't let him drive off with the money," Thomas says, taking charge of the detail.

Andy, being full of questions asks, "What's happening? Everything okay?"

Because Thomas was busy supervising his team, I answer, "Sometimes the girl has a driver walk her to the room so the john knows she's not alone, and they'll get the money so the john doesn't take it from her after they're done. Knowing the john has cash, sometimes she'll get him to open the door and then the driver will force his way in and rob the guy, certain he won't call the police."

"Here we go," says Thomas, shushing us so he could listen.

"Roger, do you have the money?" Mary asks.

"Who's this?"

"This is my driver. He'll take the money, a girl can't be too careful you know."

"Two-hundred, right?" the Colonel gets the amount on tape.

"You won't be sorry, I promise," announces Mary.

The team inside tells Thomas that the driver is leaving to go back to the car. "We'll sit on him but if he tries to leave, we'll stop him away from here, check him for the marked money and have a uniform car take him to the office. That'll keep him off the phone."

"You guys watch the driver and we'll stay with the room. When it goes down, don't bring the driver to the room. Take him to one of the uniform districts, we don't want him to know what's going on. Just let him think Mary got arrested," Thomas directs and then quiet returns to our car as we listen.

The Colonel asks what she's looking for and Mary tells him that she's just making sure he's not a cop.

"What make you think I'm a cop?"

"This guy is good," Thomas says, pleased. "He's getting the things on tape we'll need in court, we may use him again."

"Don't tell him that. He's hard enough to get along with now."

When Mary is sure he isn't the police and there's no one else in the room, they talk business. "What do you want, Roger?"

"I don't know. What can I get?"

"Well, how about getting you out of some of your clothes then and lay down on the bed. I'll get out of my clothes and join you. Then, I'll give you a rubdown and we'll work up to a happy ending."

We all hold our breath, waiting to hear how the Colonel handles this.

We hear him say, "Sounds good to me."

"That's it. Let's move one team to take the driver, the other will meet us at the room. Get the Colonel out of there and we'll meet you in the office," Thomas said, triggering the team into action.

The first team moves on the driver. One detective walks up on the passenger side window and taps on it. When the driver turns, the other detective moves to the driver side window with his badge in his hand, not giving the driver a chance to react. With both detectives having their hands on their guns, they order him to exit the vehicle slowly with his hands where they can see them. The detective pats him down and gets the marked money. They tell Thomas by radio that the driver and money are in custody and on the way to the district.

Thomas and the second team knock on room 624 saying, "Bar delivery."

"Hope you like champagne young lady," the Colonel says, recognizing Thomas' voice and sounding relieved this is almost over.

"You'll need to get that, I'm not dressed," Mary says with a flirty little smile in her voice.

When the Colonel opens the door, Detectives Thomas, Schneider and the rest of the team push into the room, while I wait in the hall. I hear Thomas tell Mary and the Colonel to get dressed, and in a few minutes the team and the Colonel appear in the hallway which is my cue to enter the room.

Looking up from her seat on the edge of bed and seeing me, Mary says, "Conway, what are you doing here? You're retired, I was at your party."

"Came along to see if I could help an old friend."

"I don't need your help, you and Thomas both know the FBI will get me out and have the charges dropped inside an hour. Besides, you have no proof, Roger and I are old friends from college," Mary said, feeling she had all the answers.

"Where do I start? First, Roger thinks your name is Wanda and the FBI won't touch you with murder charges hanging over your head. Let me introduce you to Detective Andrew Schneider, homicide," I say, hoping to get her attention.

"I didn't kill nobody, what are you trying to pull?" Mary glares at me.

Andy pulls out his notebook, opens back a few pages, looks over at her and declares, "I've got two witnesses that put you at the scene when Jack Moore was killed."

"Who's Jack Moore?" she asks him with that 'I ain't moving another step' look on her face.

"You probably know him as 'Happy Jack'," Andy says in response.

Decked out in four-inch heels and a red dress cut low in both the front and back and accessorized with a lovely pair of silver dangly earrings, Mary's demeanor changes as she is 'helped' up off the bed.

I advise her to think about what we were saying and all the trouble she was in.

****

Once at the homicide office, Thomas removes her handcuffs and asks if she'd like something to drink.

"Conway, you talk to her, you're her friend. Andy and I are going for cokes. When we return, I'll book her for prostitution and recommend that Andy charge her with complicity to commit murder." Thomas turns to face me, winks and walks out of the room, taking the roll of the bad cop.

"What's that mean? I told you I didn't kill nobody," the beginnings of fear creeping into her voice. "What're you doing to me?"

"Well, it means you might not have pulled the trigger, but you knew about it and may have helped set it up. It also means you'll go to jail, have a high bond and you'll stay in there. If you're hoping the FBI will rescue you, you're wrong. If they step in front of a murder case, they'd better have a great story for the judge, both ours and theirs. Andy's not going to play with you, this isn't about having sex for money. You understand?"

"You're lying to me about the murder and the witness and me staying in jail."

"Have you ever caught me lying to you? When I said you were going to jail, you went to jail, and when I told you I would get you out for your finals for college, I got you out. The clock's running. They have a witness that ID'd your car and picked you out of a photo pack."

Leaning down, with a hand on each arm of her chair so we were eye to eye, I challenge, "What's it gonna be?"

Jail Or Talk, Who Said We Didn't Give You A Choice?

Thomas sits the soft drink can on the edge of the table, walks to the other side, slaps an arrest pad down and flops in a chair. Andy takes the chair next to Thomas, and leaning back the same way, they both open their cokes. Tearing out one of the arrest slips, Thomas laid it down in front of Andy and hands him a pen. Andy starts writing.

"Conway, make them stop!" Mary turns to me flustered.

"You make them stop," I answer, taking an unconcerned sip of soda.

"How?" Mary is standing now, incensed about my nonchalant attitude.

 "Sit down and answer their questions."

"I told you I don't know anything," she says softly with tears in her eyes.

Andy pushes the arrest slip over to Thomas, leans back in his chair, puts his feet up on the table and crosses them. Putting both hands behind his head, he surprises everyone in the room saying, "Your car was at the scene of the shooting and you were riding in it. That information comes with witnesses." He lets that sink in and continues, "Now you can help us or, instead of making two-hundred dollars an hour with a driver, when you get out of prison you'll be standing on a cold rainy corner flagging cars and yelling, 'Hey baby, want a date'?"

Thomas turns his shocked face in towards the kid and then back at Mary and me, "He's tired and cranky because he didn't have his nap, so I'm thinking you'd better start talking or look forward to jail time."

Mary looks up at me and Andy protesting, "I didn't do anything."

"You were there, and that's all I need," Andy shoots back, taking the last drink from his can and slamming it down on the table.

"If you're protecting that dope dealer you're married to, I know for a fact he'll have your spot in the bed filled before you get changed into your orange jump suit. The DEA has pictures of him going into motels and hotels with some of your girls," Thomas says, starting to write.

"Please stop writing and I'll answer your questions, but I just can't give you information without telling the fed's first," Mary says, trying to make a deal.

"Not good enough. From this minute on, you'll speak with Detective Schneider and only Schneider," Thomas returns to writing.

"Conway, do something!" Mary screeches, with rising panic in her voice.

"The only person who can help you now is you. Anybody need another drink?" I throw my empty can in the trash and walk out the door. It's time for me to move out of the way, leaving her nowhere to hide.

I find the Colonel sitting in the sarge's office, watching the interview on the in-house monitor. He looks up, "I think she's gonna talk," like he'd been doing interviews since birth.

I pick up a can of coke, knowing this was going to be a two-coke kind of night. "We'll see," I'm not as sure of her talking as the Colonel seems to be.

Pulling a chair alongside the Colonel's, I glance over at him as we both lean back, open our cans with a pop, put our feet up on the desk and proceed to enjoy the show.

We hear Mary ask to talk to the FBI and Andy tell her she can talk to them through the plexiglass at the jail. Mary insists she wants a lawyer, and Andy repeats that she can talk to her lawyer at the jail.

Thomas asks Andy if he is finished with the arrest slip and the kid nods 'yes'. "I'll call for a car to transport her to the jail. We can call the press, do a perp walk and then the FBI will know right where to find her."

"Wait, you can't put me on TV and tell everyone I'm charged with murder," Mary objects.

"We can and we will," Thomas says.

"Where's Conway? I want to talk to Conway!" Mary demands.

"I believe he went home. Besides, you said you wanted to talk to your lawyer," Andy answers, standing and picking up the arrest slip.

"I don't need my lawyer and I'll only talk to Conway," Mary sounds as if she knows she's losing control.

Andy walks to the door and glances over his shoulder, "I'll see if he's still around."

Standing up from my place at the desk beside the Colonel; I finish the last swallow of my coke, put on my coat, get out my keys and walk across the hall into the interview room. "What do you want Mary? I'm going home and I understand you're going to jail."

"Conway, please don't let them lock me up. I'll answer their questions and tell them whatever I can," Mary cries big puppy dog tears, obvious to everyone she realizes she's let the situation get out of her control.

"You'll need to tell them everything you know, and I'd suggest you don't let them catch you in a lie," I advise her.

Settling myself on the corner of the table, I continue, "What should I tell the TV people, Thomas? They're out in the hall."

"Wait!" Mary grabs hold of me with both hands, shaking so hard that I'm shaking too. "Okay, but you'll have to protect me. They'll kill me if they suspect I talked, you don't know these people."

"Ask the lieutenant to meet me in the sergeant's office and don't talk to the press at all. If the lieutenant agrees with what I have in mind, we'll eventually have to get that thumb-sucker of a prosecutor and the DEA in here. But, not until we know the story on the killing."

I stop on my way out the door, "Mary, sit tight and we'll be right back. You need anything?"

"I'd like to go piss, wash my face and find a drink," Mary says, jumping to her feet as if it were to happen on her command. Then, taking a deep breath, she sits back down in her chair, defeated.

"We'll have a female officer take you to the restroom and you're not to go anywhere unless an officer is with you," Thomas instructs, on his way out the door.

The lieutenant arrives and I lay out my ideas. "We're going to get Happy Jack's killer, the drugs and the whole game. But, we'll have to arrange witness protection for Mary."

"Did she tell you this, Conway?"

"Lieutenant, you know better than to ask me that in front of a bunch of witnesses. But no, not yet," I said, trusting everyone in the room. "I'll tell the press there's been a change of plans and we'll get back to them. We don't need this on the six o'clock news until everything is in place. We'll have the federal prosecutor meet with us, but not tell him anything until the witness protection agreement is in place. First, let's get her on tape. This office is closed to everyone but you guys until we turn her over to the U.S. Marshals."

"I'll have the chief okay an officer to control access so we won't run into a problem with the captain," the lieutenant says adding, "Any outside questions will be referred to me. I'll call for the U.S. Attorney and speak to him before I put a prosecutor on the access list. Now, everyone call home it's going to be a long night. And order a pizza or something, we can't have our witness going hungry."

Let The Party Begin

With an officer on the door keeping everyone not on the list from entering, and the captain lurking around like a buzzard waiting for something to die, one would think everyone would be happy and excited. But the Colonel wasn't, calling me to the side and reminding me this all started over the truck driver.

"I got the street people to help you because you were gonna get the driver arrested for what he was doing to Big Charlie, and he's still taking his money. I couldn't care less about some dope dealer from Colombia or some dead tattletale. What are you gonna do about the truck driver?" The Colonel is red-faced and fighting mad.

"Did you call your sister, so she knows you're all right and will be late?" I remind him, not wanting to answer his question.

"The Deputy U.S. Attorney, two DEA agents and two marshals are in the lieutenant's office with the chief. The captain's curiosity is almost to the point of listening at the keyhole," Andy smiles, enjoying the captain's misery.

"The Colonel's not happy, Andy. Seems we ain't done nothing with the truck driver, and he is not going to let us forget."

"Sorry, in all of the excitement of the hotel and all I forgot to tell you. The detective from the downtown area took the driver into Silverman's office. They told him what they knew but they would be willing to hear his side of the story. The driver must have felt he was going to be arrested because he asked to make a deal. Silverman called the driver's boss to come down to the Hay Market. The driver eventually agreed to give Silverman two hundred dollars to pay Charlie back, after which Silverman informed him that he was barred off the lot. Then, after putting up the money and telling him he'd keep his check for it, the driver's boss fired him." The kid looked at the Colonel for approval.

"Well, that takes care of me, but I would like to stay and watch," the smile on the Colonel's face lets everyone know he feels like part of the team, and is belonging to something for the first time in a long time.

The office door opens, and the attorney comes in followed by the marshals and agents. The attorney announces that the lieutenant told him Conway and Thomas would run the case at this end.

Giving Thomas who was just getting off the phone from ordering pizza a wink, I respond, "No sir, this is Detective Schneider's case."

The kid smiles and speaks up, "The first thing we need is to get that witness protection agreement in place."

The kid takes the attorney in to sit down with Mary. We watch as he introduces himself as Mike Owens, the U.S. Attorney prosecuting Carlos, and asks her if she is willing to give a statement, sign it and testify to it in court.

After she agrees, he asks if she understands going into the witness protection program means she'll have to give up her family, friends and her name.

"That won't be hard, the only family I have is Carlos and something tells me that y'all are going to put him in jail, or maybe under it," Mary answers with a nervous smile.

Owens hands her a pen and lays a paper in front of her. "Sign here, and when the detectives have finished with you the marshals will take charge until you're given a new ID, a place to move to, and a new history."

Owens leaves the room and Andy begins the interview, "Let's get started."

"What do you want to know?" Putting her elbows on the table and a hand under her chin, Mary settles in to answer questions.

"Let's start with the night of the shooting."

"Let's start with a couple pieces of pizza and a soft drink, before the group in the other room watching us eats it all," Mary points at the hidden camera in the corner.

Andy smiles up at the camera, "You heard the lady. Make that two pieces for me." Looking back in Mary's direction, he adds, "I guess this isn't your first rodeo."

"I've been here before," she answers, ready to get the show on the road. "Carlos talked to Juan and Pedro on the front porch, telling them to bring the van to the Cook house and that Happy Jack was coming by to pick up some product." Mary stops, looks at the kid and

147

continues, "He told him to put the rat in the van and bring him to the sand pile. Where are your guys with our pizza?"

"How come you to be with Carlos that night?"

"We were going to meet another couple for dinner, after he talked to Happy Jack."

 "Did you know they were gonna kill him?"

"No, I thought they'd beat him up and leave him in the parking lot, like they did the guy they caught stealing product."

"What happened when you got to the sand pile?"

"When we got there, Juan and Pedro were standing outside the van and Carlos told me to wait in the car. I saw Juan pull Happy Jack out of the side door of the van, then he and Pedro held him by the arms while Carlos hit him a couple of times. That's when I saw Pedro hand Carlos a gun and they walked over by the sand pile. I couldn't see what was happening, but I knew something was wrong. I heard a shot and then another. Carlos came back to the van with the other guys, handed Pedro the gun and got in the car with me." Mary sits back in her chair and understands she'd crossed the line and can't go back.

"What did you do then?" asks the kid, now into the story as much for the entertainment as for the investigation.

Thomas steps into the room briefly; delivers the pizza and two cans of ginger ale and asks if they needed anything else, then leaves closing the door behind him.

"We went to dinner," Mary answers, taking a bite of pepperoni pizza.

"Did he say anything when he got back in the car?" Andy asks, picking up a piece of pizza.

Andy can see Mary is getting more relaxed as she opens her soda, "That rat won't tell the FEDs about anybody else. My guy in the federal prosecutor's office said he was telling on people for money."

"Did he say who it was that gave him the tip about Happy Jack?"

"No, he knows a lot of the people who work there from before he got fired. He said it was the best five-hundred dollars he'd ever spent."

"What did he do for the feds?"

"He was an interpreter."

"What happened next?" Andy asks, chewing a slice of pepperoni.

"Like I said, we went to dinner and we were already late."

"Let's eat our pizza and talk some more."

Now The Drugs

After the pizza is down to the end crust and the soft drinks are gone, Mary asks to go pee again. This time a marshal clears the hallway and the restroom before a female marshal walks Mary in there. When they returned, Marshal Becca Werner takes a chair in the corner under the camera. Mary takes her chair at the table and asks if she could speak to me alone. Werner said she'd have to be in the room, but would stay back.

"What do you need Mary?" I ask, sticking my head in the door.

Mary motions me closer and talking real low, she asks, "They won't let me go anywhere without them from now on, right?"

"We're going to try to keep you safe. And yes, that means being guarded by the marshals."

"I have a key in the change part of my purse. It's to a storage locker on Poplar Level Road by the expressway. There are two bags in it and they have all I'll need in them. I need to pick them up and make sure I have them before I disappear."

Behind me, I hear the door open and turn to see U.S. Attorney Mike Owens, followed by two DEA agents, but no FBI.

Mike sits down on the edge of the table and tells her one of the agents will be sitting in on the rest of her statement.

"We need you to tell the agent about the drugs and anything you know about the way they move them."

"I don't know a lot, but I'll help all I can. You guys don't know the kind of people you are dealing with," Mary says worriedly, looking Mike right in the eye.

"We know how to handle these people and I know you're scared, but you'll not go back there. Now, what I need for you to do is answer the detectives and agents questions." With that said, he walks out of the room.

Turning her back to everyone but me, Mary says quietly, "Go get my bags and then I'll tell you about the drugs."

"What's in the bags, anything illegal?" I ask, hoping she'd just tell me.

"You can look, but just you, and then bring them to me."

"Here's the deal, Mary. I'll go get the bags and bring them here before I open them. If there's anything illegal in them, you'll be charged and put out of the program." I knew that wasn't true, but I was hoping to learn what was in the bags.

"Deal," Mary announces, returning to the chair and pushing it back next to Werner.

"Tell them what they need to know and I'll go get the bags," I promise, turning back to the door.

"Not 'til you get back. Becca, how would you like to make five hundred dollars a night and not dress in those ugly pantsuits?" Mary smiles at her new marshal girlfriend.

****

With most of the late watch on the street the hallway is quiet. The captain sees me leave and makes his move to get in the room and find out what's going on. I watch as he walks to the door and reaches for the doorknob. The officer standing guard puts his hand on top of the captain's and says, "Sorry captain, you can't go in there."

"I'm the captain of this unit and I'm going in."

"Sir, the chief said if you tried to go in, I was to give you this note and tell you my orders from him were to take your badge and gun and put you in the holdover cell until he returns in the morning. His words, sir."

"I'll see about this."

"Sir, you'll have to see about it somewhere else. You can't stay here."

****

Returning from the storage locker, I place two large red gym bags on the table and glance over at Mary.

"For the last time Mary, is there anything illegal in these bags?"

"If there's nothing illegal in there, can I take them with me and not have to tell anybody?"

The U.S. Attorney, who was listening to the conversation on the monitor and wanting to know as did the rest of us what was in the bags, steps into the room. "If there's nothing illegal in the bags, you can take them with you."

"Okay, then let's get started with your questions," Mary says, moving her chair near the table and leaning over on the two bags.

"First, we have to see that there's nothing illegal in there."

"I'll show Conway, and then we can go on with the question and answers," Mary motions for everybody to leave the room.

As they walk out of the room, I know they're running to the monitor feeling superior.

"Okay, let's see what you got."

Without a word, Mary takes a paper plate from the table, dumps the pizza crumbs in the trash can, climbs up in Werner's chair and hangs the plate over the camera. Placing her finger to her lips, she whispers, "Not a word,"

I chuckle, knowing there's a lot of cussing going on at the monitor realizing they're not as smart as they thought they were.

Mary opens the first bag and I inspect it and then check the other.

Keeping my voice low, I look at Mary and ask, "Where did it come from?"

"Not a word to anybody."

I move my fingers across my lips in a sealing motion and repeat, "Not a word."

Leaning my head out the door, I yell at the guys in the office, "Nothing illegal in the bags. You guys can get started."

****

The DEA agent and the kid take their place on one side of the table across from Mary, who's facing them from the other side, and now leaning on the red bags again.

Marshal Werner removes the paper plate from the camera, then perches on her chair in the corner concentrating only on Mary's safety.

"What do you want to know?" Mary asks, stretching and assuming her little pose with her elbows on the bags and her head in her hands.

"What's in the bags?" asks Owens as we return to the sergeant's office.

I pick up a soda, take a drink and inform the room, "Nothing illegal."

We all look to the monitor and watch as the DEA agent moves his chair closer to the table and begins, "Mary, tell me how they are getting the dope into the country."

Werner shifts in her chair, leans toward the agent and comments sarcastically, "The lady will help put a big feather in your cap, the least you can do is tell her your name."

The agent looks at Werner and then at Mary, "My name is Bobby."

"Not Robert or Rob, but Bobby? How manly," she giggles and both girls burst into laughter.

Okay, Now About The Drugs

"You guys don't have a clue do you?" Mary shakes her head and smiles.

"What do you mean? We know Carlos is selling drugs and that he killed Happy Jack." Bobby was working hard to take charge.

"You don't know who shot Happy Jack, nor do you know why. You only KNOW what I've told you," Mary remarks, patting her gym bags.

"She's right, all we really know is what she told us," Andy breaks in.

Becca stands and puts her hand on Mary's shoulder, saying, "I agree. If you'd stop trying to be the almighty federal agent and listen, you might just learn something."

Sitting back in the chair, with a look on his face like a kid caught with his hand in the cookie jar, Bobby says defensively, "You don't know what I know."

"I know you think Carlos is bringing drugs in from out of the country, which tells me that Happy Jack was treating you like a mushroom. He fed you bullshit and kept you in the dark," Mary looks over at Becca to get her reaction, while leaning in closer to her two red bags.

Jumping to his feet, Bobby moves toward Mary and Andy steps in protectively, keeping him from getting too close.

Werner, now standing directly behind Mary, puts her hand on her shoulder reassuringly.

Mary looks him right in the eye as he says, "How do you know what I know?"

"Because Happy Jack was just a street level pusher, he had nothing to tell you. If he knew anything, he would have told you he wasn't importing drugs, he was importing roses."

"What are you talking about importing roses?" Bobby growls, not willing to be made to look like a fool again.

"Are you through looking at me like something you stepped in, and ready to learn what's going on?" Mary asks, without changing her expression or her tone.

Bobby takes his seat and picks up a notebook and pen. "Then let's start over, I'm a DEA agent and you can call me Bobby."

Mary stands, offering a handshake while keeping the other hand on one of the gym bags, and answers, "I'm Mary. How can I help you?"

"Tell me what you know about Carlos and the drug deals."

The tension level lowers in the interview room, as well as in the sergeant's office where "What's in the bags?" has been asked at least a dozen times.

"Tell the guys in the other room to go get more sodas and we can get started," Mary sits down and smiles at Bobby in her most ladylike expression. Andy looks directly at the camera, smiles and raises four fingers and motions for someone to go for sodas.

In the office everyone looks at one another, no one wanting to miss any part of the rose story. Finally, the Colonel sighs and speaks up saying he'd go for the drinks if someone else will buy. We all pitch in a couple of dollars and return our attention to the monitor.

"Sodas are on the way, now about the roses," Bobby begins again, leaning forward in his chair and looking at Mary over the top of the two mysterious gym bags.

"The roses are what Carlos brings into the country from Columbia. That's why y'all can't catch him," Mary leans back in her seat, now partially hidden behind the red bags.

Bobby, gritting his teeth, patiently asks, "Well, where do the drugs come from?"

"Carlos cooks them here."

"Carlos cooks the cocaine here? Where does he get the coca leafs?" Bobby looks skeptical.

"Okay, get out your paper and crayons and I'll start from the beginning," Mary says, succeeding at bringing a frown to the face of the agent.

"I'm ready to hear what you have to say," Bobby counters, takes a deep breath and brushes aside her catty remark.

"Carlos has the roses shipped into the country packed in coca leaves so the dogs don't pick up on them. Then, he sells the roses to a couple of flower shop owners he's made a deal with and some of my girls sell them on the street. It's a great cover for working the corner."

The Colonel steps into the interview room and, without a word, sits the soft drinks on the table next to the two red bags. He returns to the office and watches with us as we all concentrate on Andy handing out the drinks, then watch as he pushes his chair over near Werner. Everybody laughs, and one of the marshals asks the room as a whole if anybody thinks the kid is thinking about cocaine.

Once Mary has her drink open, Bobby starts the questioning again, "What does he do with the leaves?"

"I've only been to the Cook house once, but I watched Juan and Pedro put the leaves into a fifty-gallon drum in the garage. They added some concrete and coal oil and mixed it up with a stick and then left it to ferment." Mary was talking to Bobby, but was closely watching Andy and Becca, taking on the roll of Werner's big sister.

"Just one drum? Is that why they call it the cook house?" Bobby asks, now directing the conversation.

"I saw about four or five barrels all working leaves, and they call it the Cook house because the house belongs to a family named Cook. Oh yeah, and after they cook the stuff that comes out of the drums in the kitchen, they dry it on the basement floor," Mary says, straining to hear what Andy and Becca are talking about. "They have one of the bedrooms set up for a cutting room and another one set up for packing. The living room and dining room are set up to look like everyone else's house so that the people who come to buy or just pick up to sell on the street, like Happy Jack, never see the operation."

"Is that all you know about the Cook house and the operation?" Bobby asks, busy taking notes.

"I was only there once because that was Carlos' business. I ran my business and he ran his."

Bobby stands up, saying he needs to see if the attorney has any more questions and the kid reluctantly follows him out of the room. Mary pulls a pack of fifties from her red bag and turns, stepping close to Becca. Handing her the money, she says, "Go to the spa, have your hair and nails done and buy a little black dress. The kind that fits so tight you have to keep tugging at the hem to keep it from riding up over your hips. Then get a gold chain necklace that hangs down in layers and some come-get-me heels. Make dinner reservations at one of the best hotel restaurants, and afterwards take that kid up to one of the rooms and finish what Thomas, Conway and the Colonel have started."

"What are you talking about? I can't take this money," Becca says with a red face.

"You can take the money, it's my gift. You're a big girl, take him upstairs and scare the little boy out of him."

And Then She Was Gone

Thomas, the Colonel and myself stand watching the monitor as DEA agents and marshals follow Bobby and Attorney Owens into the interview room. Mary has her back to the door as the group files into the room. With a wave of his hand, Owens dismisses everyone but the three new marshals and Becca.

Werner takes her chair in the corner and Mary stands, sizing up the two new male marshals, one black and one white, both over six feet tall and virtual walls of muscle. Owens turns to Mary and introduces them; "This is Tom Barton" pointing first to the black officer, and then to the second, "This is John Bassett". Then turning to the female marshal, a beautiful black lady built like a model, and introduces her as Leann Baur. "She'll be your contact and will make sure you're taken care of."

"What About Becca?" Mary asks, feeling as if she needed to protect her new girlfriend.

"Werner works here and you'll see her when you return for the trial," Owens says, nodding toward Becca.

"I'm sure that Leann can hold her own in a bar fight or however you guys judge your agents, but I like Becca!" Mary's anger was apparent as she stood with her hands on her hips looking Owens in the eye.

Becca takes Mary by the shoulders and looking directly in her eyes, reassures her, "Leann is great at what she does and I guarantee you'll like her." She lowers her voice and leans in closer, "Besides, I think the Colonel is sweet on her."

Mary relaxes, smiles and pats Becca's pocket where the money is and says, "She's not the only agent around here who's turned a guy's head."

"Mary, it's time to go."

As Bassett reaches for the red bags, Mary lays both of her hands on them saying, "I'll take care of these."

"Miss Green, before we put them in the car, we have to be sure there's nothing in there that can hurt us."

"There's nothing in there that'll hurt you," Werner chimes in, adding to the assurances given to the new marshals.

"Would you mind just telling us what's in the bags?" Barton asks.

"Not at all. It's Carlos' bond money. He'd always tell the people who worked for him, that if they got arrested to keep their mouth shut and he'd get them out," Mary explains, now leaning protectively over the bags.

"But two bags?" Bassett asks.

Mary opens both bags. "It takes two bags."

Mike Owens, the three agents and Werner, seeing the bundles of money sorted with a rainbow of different colored bank bands, all ask in unison, "How much is in there?"

"I haven't counted it, but I figure it's around two-million dollars, give or take a few thousand," Mary answers, winking at Werner.

"Carlos and company are going to be disappointed this time tomorrow," smirked Tom Barton, picking up the two bags after looking to Mary for permission and moving to the door.

"The car is downstairs in the garage, time to go," Leann reminds everybody. Then, putting her hand on the small of Mary's back, urges her towards the door and her new life.

The Colonel, Thomas, Andy, Bobby and myself are waiting in the hall when the door opens, and the group drifts out. Leann patiently stops with Mary as she hugs everybody and says her goodbyes with tears welling up in her eyes.

The two male agents wait at the elevator while Werner hands a card to Andy, and with her hand to the side of her face makes the 'call me' sign. When the kid looks at the back of the card, he sees that her cell number is handwritten alongside a little smiley face. The Colonel asks Leann if they could have coffee when she gets back in town and she smiles and nods. The elevator doors close and they're gone; leaving the rest of us staring at the doors, not wanting to move.

After a slow walk back to the office Owens announces, "Time to get to work. Get the agents out on the Cook house. See if you can find Carlos, Juan and Pedro and watch them, so when we move on the operation we'll know where to find them."

"What about us?" Thomas asks.

"Yeah, after all it is our case," Andy grumbles.

"Well, yes, you guys will all be a big part of this. You'll be there for the arrest," Owens says, patting Thomas on the back.

"Turn around and I'll check your back for knife wounds," I turn and look Mike Owens in the eye. "What part will we play in the case?"

"What would you guys like to do?"

"I want to lead the team that arrests Carlos," Andy is quick with his answer.

"You got it."

Once everybody has checked their messages, it's time to go to work. The SWAT team is called out for 6:00 am and a judge is called to set up a time to sign the warrant. DEA starts out to drive by and get a description of the Cook house while the FBI leaves to sit across the street, where they can watch the comings and goings of the house and the garage. The fire department is put on standby.

I'll ride with Andy, and the Colonel will be in the car with Thomas. The first stop for both cars is White Castle for coffee. Two cups for each man; one for now, one for later. Adrenaline can be measured by the bucketful and the coffee will give us something to do with our hands.

The Circus

After four hours of staring at a dark house and Carlos' red Mercedes, the hardest part of staying awake on a detail is now peeking over the trees through the windshield. As the bright light tortures our tired eyes, the silence is broken by the FBI radio on the seat when

Bobby checks in to make sure everyone's in place. Once we have an eyeball on the key players, we'll move.

Andy sits up in his seat and excitedly informs us and the radio, "A light just came on in the upstairs window," and just like that, the need to empty our bladder and scratch our butts pass as the adrenaline is now leaking out of our ears.

The radio announces that Juan and Pedro have just arrived in a brown van at the Cook house across town. We count eight Hispanics; six males and two females all dressed in the uniform of the day, jeans and sweatshirts.

"Any sign of Carlos?" Bobby is now wide awake.

"Got a light on upstairs. Looks like he's up and moving," Andy answers.

"Are you sure it's him?"

"No, but his car's still out front."

"Wait! Everybody sit still. Pedro is putting the signs on the truck, looks like they've got a delivery at the airport," Bobby barks into the radio.

"Carlos is getting in the Mercedes," Andy reports, trying to sit still and not fidget.

****

The DEA car following the van lets everyone know that the van has just returned from the airport. We watch as it backs into the driveway and two of the men open the garage doors and start unloading boxes from the back of the truck. They take the roses from the boxes and place them in five gallon buckets and then dump the boxes of leaves into the barrels.

162

The red Mercedes pulls up in front and Carlos climbs out and walks to the garage where the Hispanic males are working.

"Everyone in place and ready, but stand by, we got kids at the bus stop. We can't take a chance on anything going wrong," Bobby says, in a calm tone.

You could feel the tension in the car. Andy already has his door half-open as we watch the teens get on the school bus, laughing without a care in the world. As soon as the bus turns the corner, the radio barks the order "GO!"

The quiet street becomes a scene from a movie as one SWAT truck pulls up in the alley and the other one rolls to a stop in the middle of the street directly in front of the Cook house. The doors fly open almost before they come to a stop and two teams, eight men each, jump from the rear of each truck. The first team from the truck out front runs to secure the garage and the driveway side of the house while the other team moves to the front door. The two teams in the alley move to the back door and the far side of the house. Nobody is going anywhere.

The SWAT team's radio triggers the action and simultaneously the garage door lifts and the front and back doors of the house fly open. The workers in the garage with Juan and Pedro are all pushed to the floor, checked for weapons and handcuffed. Carlos tries to makes a run for the door, but is grabbed by his arm and thrown up onto the counter, landing in the sink with the dirty dishes. The team from the front door clear the upstairs and return with the two women in cuffs.

With the workers sitting on the floor in the garage, Carlos is stashed in a chair at the dining room table where two FBI agents are already recording the evidence. Carlos is dripping dishwater everywhere and has what I figure is coffee grounds in his hair and on his face. He's demanding his "abogado" and telling everyone he'll be out by morning and have our jobs.

"Why does he want an avocado?" Andy asks puzzled.

"Not an avocado, kid. An abogado is Spanish for lawyer," Thomas laughs.

The Colonel laughs and counters, "I don't have a job for you to take and if you're counting on the bail money in the storage bin, boy do you have a surprise coming!"

"Did you thieves take my money? You can't steal my money!" Carlos yells, trying to stand, but is pushed back down by the SWAT member who put him in the sink. She now has her helmet off so everyone can see her long red hair. She looks familiar.

"We didn't steal your money, Mary got it," Andy chuckles.

Carlos, trying to stand again yells, " Both bags?"

"Yeah, she got both bags."

"Then, she'll get me out," Carlos says, smiling.

"I don't think so, Carlos. She's with the marshals in WITSEC. You'll see her again in court," Andy is beside himself.

"She took the whole two million? That bitch!" Carlos is again trying to get to his feet and, once again adding insult to injury, he's put back in his chair by the young female SWAT member who reminds me of Mary; young, but experienced and professional about what she does.

"We got everything we need," the agent at the table says, picking up the copies of the search warrant with the list of things that was taken. He rolls up a copy of the warrant and pushes it into Carlos' still wet shirt pocket.

164

With the drug manufacturing and delivery service closed down, and the boss and his employees on their way to jail, someone suggests that a celebration breakfast is in order.

Thomas is thinking about a beer, but being only nine in the morning the bars aren't open. "Let's get a six-pack and go over behind the flood wall," he says, looking at the group.

"I can't drink beer, but maybe something else," says the Colonel.

"We'll get you and the kid some milk," Thomas smirks.

"Stop calling me the kid! I just took down one of the biggest drug dealers in this town!"

"I think he's earned the right to be called by his last name, like you guys," the Colonel defends his new buddy.

"Okay, Schneider it is. Welcome to the club and it's your turn to buy," Thomas says with a slow smile, letting us know he remembers his first nine o'clock beer behind the flood wall.

"I'm gonna pull into this 'stop and rob' to pee. Schneider, get a six-pack of Bud and whatever the Colonel's drinking," he says, looking over at the kid.

Now feeling a part of the group, Schneider is off to the beer box when the Colonel yells, "Look, we're on the news!"

From the TV mounted on the wall behind the cashier, a female reporter is interviewing U.S. Attorney Mike Owens in front of the Federal Courthouse. We all stop to listen as she says, "After months of investigation the DEA, along with the FBI, was able to make an arrest and stop one of the largest drug dealers in this part of the country."

"They didn't even say we helped," Andy howls, about to throw the beer at the TV.

"Budget time in Washington, son," I tell him in my most fatherly tone.

****

After quietly drinking our breakfast behind the flood wall, Andy asks the Colonel and myself where we could be found if they need our help again.

"On the liar's bench in the bus stop at Second and Jefferson, on warm days. But if the weather's bad, we'll be in our office at the Starbucks across the street in the hotel. Of course, we have breakfast at the Days Inn down the street a couple times a month," answers the Colonel.

Thomas smiles at the kid as he throws his empty bottle in the trash can. "Schneider, my boy, you just earned a front row seat to the greatest show on earth."

The Colonel, slipping back in to the old habit of checking the garbage can, yells, "I want a front row seat at the trial."

Here We Go Again

Rain beating again the window wakens me as daylight adds shadows to the bedroom. A sleepy glance at the clock lets me know Maureen is already up and hurrying about, getting ready for work. After pouring my ever present cup of coffee, I move to the room we call the office to stay out of her way and to decide how to spend this rainy day.

There are cases you catch in your career that go unsolved, investigations that pull at you like an itch you can't reach as you try to fall asleep. If you're a detective worth your salt, these go with you when you retire. Sitting at my desk, still in my PJs and staring out the rain-covered window, I can hear my personal nightmare laughing at me from the bookshelf.

I look for something on the television; news which is depressing, weather that I can get through the window, cartoons, and infomercials which promise you can buy something that will make you slimmer, taller, or smarter.

From the big blue binder on the shelve behind me I hear, *"Will today be the day you put me to rest?"*

Like dozens of times before, I pull the case file from the shelf and place it, unopened, in front of me on the desk. Picking up my cup I walk to the kitchen to get a refill, but I know I'm going back to the binder. I take a sip of black coffee, return to the office and open it. The first page hits me as hard this time as every time before; the wanted poster with a sketch of a young black male with the words in bold letters, **'Wanted for the Murder of Jennifer Barnes on December 3rd.**

I close my eyes and go back in time as I remember Jenny's friend Sue, who was working the bank drive-thru, a stand alone booth in the parking lot. When she could stop crying and catch her breath, she began, "Jenny was leaving work early and going to stop by my booth to give me a key to her house so that I could feed Biscuit."

"Who's Biscuit?" I asked, trying to keep her talking.

"Biscuit is their dog. They had plans to go visit Bob's family for Christmas this weekend and her family next weekend, so their son would be home for Christmas morning. She was singing a Christmas carol coming across the lot," Sue broke down, lowering her head and looking at the floor.

"Take your time. Do you need a drink of water or a coke?" I asked, placing my hand reassuringly on her shoulder.

"No, I'm okay, what can I tell you?" Sue sobbed, already openly missing her friend.

"Was there anyone else in the parking lot, anyone in a car at your booth?" I asked her again, to get her statement flowing.

"There were three or four people walking back from lunch when this kid runs up out of nowhere and pushed Jenny against a car. He pointed a gun at her and tried to pull the bank bag out of her hand."

I remember Sue standing and starting to pace in the small room.

Backing up to the door to give her as much room as I can, I continued, "Why did she have a bank bag? Was she bringing you money?"

"No, she keeps her keys, some money and pictures of her son in it so she didn't have to carry her purse in the bank. I bet that kid thought she had money. He pulled at the bank bag and she fought to hang on and that's when the gun went off. The young man ran and Jenny walked to my door and fell on the floor."

****

Maureen comes into the office, kisses me on the forehead and tells me she is leaving for work. Glancing at the binder on my desk, she shakes her head and remarks, "Not that again, Ray. Glad I'm going to work."

After walking her downstairs to the front door, I stop in the kitchen to, once again, refill my coffee cup and return upstairs to the binder.

168

Systematically, I lay out the mug shots and copies of the NCIC reports for the subjects we suspect of being involved, in stacks across the desk in front of me. After sitting all the dust collectors on the floor, I tape the pictures of the crime scene to the closet door and place the statements of the subject on the top of the bookcase under the window.

"Wait, where's my white board?"

Poking around, I locate it behind the corner bookshelf.

Moving the desk chair to the middle of the room like the captain on Star Trek, I'm finally ready and this time starts like all the times before. Holding my cup in both hands, I lean back in my chair and stare at the pictures, hoping I'll see something I've haven't seen before.

The phone rings and I see it's Schneider. I hope he doesn't tell me he has cleared the case, because I'll have to go back to working on another way to waste my day, like take a nap. "Hey, Andy, what's the police department got my favorite kid detective working on today?" Sitting up, I gulp a huge drink of hot coffee and wait for the caffeine to hit my system.

"Can you and the Colonel meet me at the coffee shop at Third and Jefferson?" Andy asks, stress evident in his voice.

"I'll call the Colonel, but we can meet here at the condo. What's going on?"

"Not over the phone. I need to bring a couple of people with me, will that be okay?"

"Good guys or bad guys?" I wonder out loud.

"Becca and her boss. He has questions for you. That okay?"

"Becca is always welcome. As far as her boss, he can't be any worse than the Colonel. If you guys want anything but coffee, bring it with you," I tell him, hoping it'll be a short meeting and they'll be gone before Maureen gets home.

I hang up and immediately call the Colonel, "What's going on, Colonel?"

"Busy on the farm, what about you?"

"The kid called and wants us to meet with him, Becca, and her boss. You need a ride?"

"Nah, I'll drive the farm truck. Where are we going to meet them?"

"My condo in an about an hour," I answer, knowing Maureen will have a fit when she finds out I had all these people in the condo without cleaning it or getting in snacks.

"I'll be there."

After hanging up the phone, I get dressed, make the bed and make a fresh pot of coffee. It's raining outside, I'm not going anyplace and now I have to get out of my pj's before noon.

****

The doorbell rings and spotting an ugly, faded-green pickup truck in the parking space in front of the garage, I look around to find the Colonel standing there in a pair of jeans with a torn knee and a gray tee-shirt with paint on the front.

Thinking back to the first time I saw him, I chuckle, noting that he dressed better when he was drunk and homeless. Opening the storm door, I get him inside before anyone spots him, although the truck will drive the neighbors nuts. Before I can get the door closed, the kid's unmarked car pulls up in front and Andy throws the flashing blue light up on the dashboard, leaving the car parked in the street. I can feel neighbors peeking out their windows and know my phone will ring shortly. One of them is bound to call Maureen, tattling on me like I'm a teenager having friends over when the parents are gone.

Andy starts talking on the short way to the porch, "Marshal Baur has been shot and Marshal Barton is dead." The Colonel stops halfway up the stairs and turns asking, "Leann was shot? I just talked to her two days ago."

Still at the door, I welcome the only person in the group I don't know. As we shake hands, he introduces himself as Marshal Ron Adams, Director of WITSEC.

Once in the living room, Becca and the kid settle on the sofa next to one another. Adams and the Colonel take a seat in the two kitchen chairs I've moved in, leaving the recliner for me.

"I have a busy day, so what can we do for you Marshal?" asks the Colonel, causing everyone in the room to look at this rag bag.

Ron stands, loks around and takes charge of the group saying, "We think we've got a leak in the U.S. Attorney's office and we need your help."

"I know, just don't tell them anything," the Colonel remarks, returning from the kitchen holding his coffee cup with both hands.

"That's a great idea, but we need to talk to them, to keep them in the loop until we locate the leak," Becca pipes in.

"Sounds like a job for the FBI, not that they could find shoes in a shoe box," I add, not wanting to miss a chance for a dig at the feds.

"We want you and the Colonel to bring Mary back to Louisville," Ron pulls his chair up next to my recliner.

Adams now has the Colonel's attention, "Were you rocked too hard when you were little?"

"No, this has been approved by the DOJ. I can't give you a badge, but I will give you a letter from the marshal's office that you can use if things go wrong," Adams replies.

"I don't want a badge, I want a cape," the Colonel demands, posing; chest out, feet apart, and hands on his hips like a superhero.

Trust Not In Everyone's Heart

Ron's phone interrupts. He pulls it from his pocket and turning his back to the group walks to the kitchen. The room gets quiet with everyone trying to hear what's being said. There's a lot of "Yes sirs" and "no sirs", but no real information. It ends with a "Goodbye, sir" and he returns to the room.

Smiling and looking at the Colonel, he remarks, "I can't authorize a cape, but if you'd like to tie a bed sheet around your neck and promise not to jump off the garage roof while trying to fly, it would be okay."

The room erupts in laughter and a team is born.

Andy adds the Colonel will have to get matching jockey shorts and Becca adds a wife-beater tee shirt with a big 'C' on the front.

"Well, I'm not riding with him dressed like that," I laugh, piling on.

Ron brought the group back around to business, to the relief of the Colonel, saying, "Time to get serious."

Everyone sits down and we all turn our attention to Ron, who was standing in front of the fireplace like he might break into song and dance. Well, everyone but the Colonel who was still thinking about his special 'super-Colonel' outfit.

"I've assembled a collection of various plans for us to work on. First thing is we don't tell the U.S. Attorney's office anything until we have Mary safely here. But that won't help find the leak."

"But it would keep her safe, and that is our job," Becca reminds us.

"I'm hoping with your help to do both," Ron was ready for the questions, letting everyone know he had spent time analyzing the problem.

Looking at Adams and waiting to see how they'd fit into the plan, everyone mapped out their own preferences. Some wanted to be part of the group to get Mary back safe and some wanted to be on the team stopping the leak.

"There will be three teams; one will be moving Mary to court and one will be setting the trap for the hitman," Ron says, starting to pace.

"What about the third team? Are they going to man the phones?" The Colonel asks from in front of the sliding glass doors, still working on his superhero pose.

"The third team is the bait for the trap; the decoy, a team to bring the hitman out in the open. I've got more people coming in to help from out of state. Conway, the Colonel and Becca will move Mary from her location to the safe house. Andy, you and three guys from the vice team will be the trap. Myself, a marshal from the Boston office and two female marshals from Tennessee will be the decoy. We'll need a place to meet and work from," Adams says.

My phone rings and caller ID tells me it's Maureen. "Hello Sweetie, I was just getting ready to call you."

"JoAnn called and said there's a ratty looking truck and a police car with several people in front of the house," Maureen says, not sounding pleased. "Anything I need to know?"

"Nah, it's just the Colonel and some police friends. Everything's okay," I assure her, trying to sound upbeat.

"The house is not clean and isn't the Colonel your wino friend?" she asks, warily.

"Yes dear, he was a wino at one time but not now, and I picked up before they got here," I reply, with a voice reeking of 'little boy'.

"Well, I'm getting calls like when your police pals had the horse tied to the tree out front."

"I promise they won't shit in the driveway like the horses, well maybe the Colonel, but I'm pretty sure he's housebroke," I laugh, trying to ease the tension. "See you in a while."

"Everything okay?" Ron asked, with everyone looking at me for an answer.

"Sure, I'm the king in my castle."

"When the queen is at work," Becca jokes, causing the group to erupt in laughter.

174

"Becca's team, you and the Colonel will pick Mary up at the place where we've hidden her and then drive her back to the safe house here. Becca will be called to start in a direction and be given the pickup point once she is clear of the city and we're sure she's not being followed. Andy's team, Thomas and his crew will cover you and set the trap. I'll see that the U.S. Attorney's office gets the info we want them to have, and I'll meet the out-of-town team," Ron stops talking long enough to ask for a cup of coffee.

The Colonel offers to get it and Ron continues, "I'll give Becca's team enough time to get clear, and then put out the information like we always do."

"Why did you ask the Colonel and myself to be a part of this? You've got thousands of marshals you can call on." I'm having a bad feeling about this.

"Hey, you guys know Mary and she knows you."

"You're going to put an old tired detective who thinks rules are for fools and a street drunk who reduces the per capita income in whatever zip code he's in, to protect a key witness?" I challenge, looking him in the eye.

"He's one of the good guys, you can trust him," Becca interjects, coming to the defense of her boss.

"You're in the car with Mary, along with two people who can be blamed if things go wrong," I bark at Becca and Ron.

"What do you want from me, damn it! Mary won't testify if you three are not the ones that move her," Ron finally tells us the reason he wants us in.

"I'll get back to you with our plans after we have a chance to talk it over," I tell him, ending the meeting as I pick up my cup and head for the kitchen.

175

Trust Comes Slow, But It Comes

Once everyone is out of the way and only the Colonel is left saying goodbye at the door, I confide, "I don't trust Ron Adams. He's a federal cop and one fed is like another. But, Beccca does trust him and she works with him every day. We need to find out about him. What if he's the leak and is sitting us up to get Mary killed? If they shoot up the car in an ambush, there's no one that they have to worry about." Putting my arm around the Colonels shoulder, I walk him to the truck.

With a wary glance at my arm on his shoulder he asks, "What 'cha you got in mind?"

"I'm going to check with Thomas. He and his team are going to be a part of this, maybe he knows Adams."

After waving good bye to the Colonel, I call Thomas and ask if he is working, and if he can meet me. His team is working at Third and York near the library and he tells me to come on down. He also warns me to not try to pick up the blond on the corner, she's a cop.

****

Walking back and forth in front of the library, and waiting for one of the gentleman who spend their lunch hour looking for female companionship instead of soup and a sandwich, is the blond. The undercover van, marked 'Uncle Joe's Plumbing' pulls to the curb and Thomas tells me to get in.

"The geek in the back, with the headset and tape recorder, is Detective Tracy Ball. I'll introduce you to the other two detectives on the team when we take a break."

Tracy hollers, "Got one on the line."

Thomas puts his headset on and points to another set on the dashboard, motioning me to put them on. Though the headset I can hear a man's voice saying, "Hi young lady, I've never seen you out here before."

As the detective leans into the car, she flirts, "I'm new on this corner, handsome."

Thomas looks over and smiles, "Now the dance on the corner begins."

The man starts, "Do you have a place?"

"Yeah, the San Antonio Inn, a block over."

"How much?"

"You tell me."

"You ain't a cop are you?"

"Do I look like a cop?" the detective laughs, standing with her hands on her hips and pushing her chest out.

"I got twenty-five dollars."

From the back of the van, Tracy remarks, "I got twenty-five dollars."

"I'll walk, you drive and I'll meet you in front of 110. I don't want any police to see me get in the car."

"Hurry, I'm on my noon break.

"Time to go, you riding along?" Thomas turns to me.

"You bet. You guys are getting ready to ruin his lunch hour."

Tracy yells from the back, "We're going to ruin more than his lunch."

"Don't feel sorry for him, these guys cruise around here at noon and hit on the high school girls coming to the library, or the ones going to one of the hamburger places to hang out. There was even a report from a middle-aged lady with a bag of groceries at the bus stop."

When we pull up in front of the motel, we see the blond walk up to the door and the guy get out of his car, looking around as if he was scared his wife would jump out from behind a bush. The blond opens the door, and the guy looks around once more, then goes inside.

"This is the best part," Tracy smiles.

Through the body mike that the blond is wearing, we hear a man's voice say, "Sir, you're under arrest for soliciting prostitution." The door flies opens as the man rushes out, but Thomas, Tracy and myself are standing in his way.

Stepping back and sitting on the corner of the bed, he puts his head down and starts to cry, "Please don't arrest me, I'll lose my job at the phone company, my wife will leave me and I'll be ruined. This is the first time I've ever done this."

"Ray, meet Detective Meredith Rhodes, she's new with the unit. The ugly guy in the corner that looks more like a doper than a cop is Willy Basset.

Motioning me back out of the room, Thomas asks, "What is it you want to talk about?"

"Do you know the marshal who's running the detail to bring Mary back for trial?"

"Yeah, we all know him, he's one of the good guys. How do you know about the detail, its top secret."

178

"The Colonel and I are on the pickup team with Becca."

"Okay. Well, you can trust Adams. It was one of his people that got shot and another killed because of the leak, so you can bet he wants the person who set them up. The hard job will be to make sure he doesn't kill the leak before we find out who's paying for the info."

"Leann was the one who got shot and she and the Colonel have a thing, I think. He didn't take the news well, so we may have our hands full with him too."

"Then lets get Mary back safe and lock up a federal employee," he answers, as the motel group passes by escorting the man from the phone company to the police car.

Time To Bring Mary Home

The next two days I'm a stay at home husband; cleaning, laundry, dishes and having dinner ready promptly at seven. After going to the gym in the mornings, I nap and then watch a little television. Today, after returning from the gym, I find an envelope taped to the storm door. All I can think of is what has the HOA decided that I've done wrong now. Pulling the paper off the door and pitching it on the table, I head to the living room because it's time for 'COPS', one of my favorite shows. With a cup of coffee in hand, I sink into my easy chair and life is good.

My pocket rings and I remove my phone to check the caller ID. It's the Colonel. "How are things down on the farm?" I ask, without a hello.

"Some guy with a badge gave Deana an envelope with the words, 'The Colonel', written on the front."

"Did you open it?"

"Sure I opened it."

"Well, read it to me."

"Colonel, pack an overnight bag. It's time to bring Mary back. You need to pick up Becca behind the cinemas on Bardstown Road at 7pm. Use the old farm truck and Becca will tell you where to go. Ron."

Tearing open the envelope from my front door, I read into the phone, *"Ray, meet me near the pool at the Holiday Inn on Jefferson Street around 7pm. Bring an overnight bag. Time to bring Mary back. Ron."*

"Well, Colonel, I guess I'd better tell Maureen I'm gonna be playing cowboys and Indians for the next couple days."

"Okay, I guess we get the facts as we go cause Ron is not giving anyone the information needed to see the overall plan. See you when I see you. Be safe, be careful," the Colonel reminds me as the line goes dead.

After packing a bag, I go by Maureen's office to tell her that I'll be working with the marshals for a couple of days and will call when I can. "The marshal's office, short two homeless drunks," Maureen retorts, kissing me goodbye and cautioning me to be careful. She's an old hand at this and knows to send me off with a smile, even with a heart full of worry.

I pull in the parking lot of the Holiday Inn near the pool and open the driver door to get out, just as Ron steps from between nearby cars. "Thanks for picking me up, I wasn't sure you trusted me enough to show up," Ron mutters, climbing in the passenger seat.

"I checked on you and was told you were one of the good guys and you wanted the people that shot up some of your marshals."

Ron looks me in the face for the first time and says, "Drive to the Colonel's farm."

"The Colonel's farm?"

"Here's the key to the green Ford over there, the car you'll use later to pick up Mary" he says, pointing at a car parked by the pool and dropping the keys in the cup holder.

"Still don't really understand why you're using the Colonel and me to move a witness when you have a whole office full of agents," I challenge, as I turn onto the interstate.

He thinks for a minute and then answers, "A couple of good reasons, actually. We have a leak and it might be coming from our office. The other is that after the shooting, Mary said she won't come to court unless you two are part of her protection team. The people in the federal government that know the plan talk, and if the leak is smart, they can put the pieces together and we lose more agents. But, if the leak can't get the info from talking to the other agents, they'll try to follow myself and Becca. We're counting on them not knowing about you guys, and everyone in the U.S. Attorney's office already knows you don't like to be around feds, much less work with them."

"That sounds okay, but if they're following Becca, you just burned the Colonel having him pick her up."

"They followed Andy and Becca to the movie and watched them go inside, so they're sitting on Andy's police car. Andy is still in the theatre, but Becca changed into her gym clothes and went out the back door where the Colonel was waiting in an ugly farm truck. In an hour or so, Andy will come out of the movie with Agent Simone Torres wearing Becca's clothes and they'll go to Becca's apartment. Once inside, they'll wait about an hour and turn off all the lights except the bedroom light. The tail will relax, thinking they're in for the night. You and I will pick Andy up in the alley, leaving the tail out front watching his car. In a few minutes, Simone, now wearing a pair of running shorts, baseball cap and tank top will do her stretching exercises, making sure that the tail has something to stare at besides what her face looks like. Then, she'll jog off down the street and around the corner where she'll get in her car and drive off to meet us at the farm."

"What about the people that may be following you?"

"They won't follow me on the street once I leave the office. I supervise four teams, but I never go to the safe house or handle a witness. The information they get from me will come from going though my desk and I'll make sure they find what they want, when I want them to find it. Now, let's go rescue Andy from behind Becca's apartment."

"Glad you're on our side."

"Yep, me too. We'll be heading to an apartment over the horse barn at the Colonels place. Once the move starts, the Louisville SWAT team will secure the farm. His family will be out of town, something they already had planned. Deana and Joe know what's going on and have for a couple days now."

"They knew and didn't say anything. I've always said you can't trust them rich white people," I say, laughing an adrenaline laugh.

****

The whole drive, from picking up Andy behind the apartment and then all the way to the barn, goes without a word. Ron is busy writing and checking notes in a file while Andy changes into blue jeans and a polo in the back seat.

Pulling up between the barns, I see a half dozens cars and the farm truck. Lights in the apartment are on as well as the night lights in the stalls. We're the last to arrive.

Upstairs, Thomas and his team are watching *Big Bang Theory*. Becca, Meredith, and a lady I would soon learn is Simone are in the kitchen checking the cabinet for snacks and laughing like schoolgirls.

Ron says, loud enough for everyone to hear, "Can you guys come in the living room and turn the TV off. This will be the last time we meet, so listen up. The move will start tonight and this will be the command post. For safety purposes, I'll be the only one to know the pickup points and location of the safe house. All info will be on a need to know basis. Becca, your team will be Conway and the Colonel and I'm really sorry about that. You'll pick Mary up tonight."

"Where are we going?" I ask, just beating out the Colonel.

"I'll tell you when we're on the road," Becca answers.

"Andy and Simone, you two will meet Marshals Donna Burghardt and Reece Rooney in Nashville, Tennessee and start back for Louisville at noon tomorrow. Just don't let the Irish guy use the radio, I can't understand a damn word he says. Thomas, your team will take four vehicles and trail Andy and Simone to Nashville. You'll be their cover on the way back to Louisville. Once Mary is in the safe house, I'll leave the file on my desk and return here. Then, I'll call the U.S. Attorney, telling him we are moving Mary from Tennessee and will be in the hotel by five o'clock. Any questions? Let's get the job done."

A Hooker For Daddy

After the hugging and shaking of hands and wishing everyone good luck is over, we load up the cars and start for points unknown to all but Ron.

Becca, the Colonel and I jump into the rust and primer colored farm truck. The Colonel takes the driver seat and I help Becca up in the cab, still dressed in her sweatpants and a pullover. Sliding in and rolling down the window, I realize that the air conditioning works only in spits and fits.

Becca jokes, "When you see three people in a pickup truck, do you know how you can tell which one is the real cowboy?"

The Colonel, looking over his shoulder to back the truck out of the parking space asks, "How?"

"They're the one in the middle. They don't have to drive and they don' t have to get out to open the gate."

On the half hour drive to the Holiday Inn we laugh and catch up on what has been going on with one another. The Colonel asks Becca if she is still dating the kid and if him going to Tennessee with Simone worries her.

"Nope, I'm not like that. I trust him."

The Colonel continues to poke, "She's one good looking gal, did you see those long legs?"

Thank God that we arrive at the hotel before there's gun play.

Once in the parking lot, the bags are put in the trunk of the green Ford and the Colonel parks the truck in a far corner of the parking lot. Becca suggests we leave while he's gone.

She jumps in the drivers seat and I call shotgun, so the Colonel climbs in the middle of the backseat when he gets back. He perches on the edge of the seat so that his head is almost in the front seat between us.

Since Becca and the Colonel are still not speaking, I ask the first question of the trip, "Where are we going from here?"

"My dad's fishing lodge at Rough River," Becca answers.

"Hey, wish you'd said something. I didn't bring my fishing pole. But then, I'm not sure we have time for a day at the lake," said the Colonel.

"Mary is staying with my dad and his fishing buddy at the lake. Ron and I didn't think anyone would look for her there."

"You got your dad a hooker for his weekend at the lake? What a great daughter you are!" laughs the Colonel, sliding back in his seat.

"I didn't get my dad a hooker! I hid a witness there for a couple of weeks and my dad and his friend agreed to keep an eye on her!"

"Your dad is a big boy and I hope that he and his friend had a great time," I interject, trying to defuse the tension in the car that's quickly getting out of hand.

"You're right, Conway. You got a gun?" Becca asks.

"You bet your ass I got a gun. I don't go nowhere around the feds without a gun," I answer, patting my shoulder holster under my coat.

"What about you Colonel, you got a gun?" Becca asks sweetly, speaking to him for the first time since we left the farm.

"I don't own a gun, but I think there's one here behind you," the Colonel tells her, while pulling an automatic from the pocket behind the seat.

The rest of the two-hour drive to the fishing camp is filled with childlike questions; "Did you see those cows", "Can we stop, I got to pee", "I want something to drink", and "Are we there yet?" mostly coming from the backseat, as the Colonel takes the place of an over anxious three-year-old.

After about an hour into the trip, Becca breaks the silence, "I hope my dad is all right. He's been by himself since my mom passed about four years ago. Mary is twenty years his junior and wilder than the women he meets at the senior center or the church bingo."

"You may be surprised young lady, what your dad does and doesn't do," adds the Colonel, taking a break from, "Are we there yet?"

Becca, back on offense says, "My dad is a good man."

"Get your panties out of a bunch; good, bad, or indifferent, he's a man, little lady," I butt in, trying again to bring peace to the long drive. I feel like a kindergarten teacher as we pull into the last service station before the cabin, refuel and take a restroom break.

The Colonel and Becca refuse to speak to each other for the last leg of the trip. I welcome the quiet while I think of the ways this could all go south.

From the service station to the cabin takes about forty-five minutes. There we find Mary, Dad, and his buddy, sitting on the front porch. Becca's dad and Mary are in the swing and his buddy is in the rocker.

"Looks like they're resting up after a tiring game of bingo to me," the Colonel declares, opening the door to get out and trying his best to push Becca's buttons.

Mary is instantly out of the swing and reaching the car, hugs Becca first, then the Colonel and then me, like a grandma welcoming her grandchildren home for Thanksgiving. Dad and his friend are only a few steps behind.

Once Becca has introduced everyone, Dad tells us the grill is working and if we have time to eat, they could put some burgers on. But, Becca tells Mary to get her things because we need to start for Louisville right away, in order to get back before dark. The Colonel smirks in the background.

While the Colonel takes Mary's suitcase to the car, Becca hugs her dad, trying to stay between him and Mary with a 'he's my daddy' look on her face. Mary, however, is not to be blocked out and the scene quickly resembles two basketball players pushing for a spot under the basket.

The Colonel, Dad's fishing buddy and I lean against the car, just watching the show.

Finally, with Dad's help, we're able to get Becca and Mary into the back seat. I have a strong urge to disarm everyone in the car, but the best I can do is move the Colonel's gun safely to the front seat under the armrest.

"I had the best time with your dad and his friend, this was a great idea," Mary says, not seeming to be worried about what waits for her when we get back.

"What did you guys do for two weeks?" Becca asks, with a 'I want to kill you' smile, but I'm thinking she really wants to ask if Mary had screwed her dad.

"They were so nice, we went out on the boat and they tried to teach me to fish. I laid out on the deck and just look at my tan," Mary giggles, pulling down the waistband of her shorts to show her tan line.

The Colonel turns to ask, "Well, did you catch any fish?"

Mary ignores the Colonels question and continues, "One night we went to the lodge to eat and some ladies that had their eye on your dad and his friend came by the table to give me the once over, asking if I was a daughter. When they were looking, I just rubbed on the guys and kissed them on their cheeks. We had some wine and laughed until they all left. Then there were other guys who stopped by the cabin and your daddy told me they came by to see me, because they had never stopped by for a beer before. We went to town, and I brought the littlest bikini I could get into and spent my time laying out on the back deck. We were the talk of the river."

"Oh yes, and to answer the question you won't ask me, I didn't sleep with your dad. They were perfect gentlemen," Mary stage whispers to a contrite Becca.

Still openly unhappy, Becca scolds, "You were there to stay safe, not draw attention to yourself, so that the people trying to kill you couldn't find you. You endangered yourself, my dad, his friend and all the people around the lodge."

"Slow down, missy. This place has better protection than the marshals who, by the way, almost got me killed. If I ran my business here and not Louisville, you guys would never have caught me."

"What are you talking about?" Becca snaps back.

"We knew when you stopped at Dan's Gas Station. You went to the restroom, the white guy put gas in the car and the black guy got soft drinks for y'all. When Edna's daughter had her baby up north, we knew it was a girl before it was cleaned and given to its momma. If someone new came to the area, we would have known," Mary smiles, putting a hand on Becca's shoulder. The tension in the car lowers considerably, but Becca is still not talking to the Colonel.

The rest of the trip is spent with the girls chatting about Andy, "Are y'all still seeing each other?" "Is it serious?"

Now that they are talking like two college roommates, I can start worrying about what's waiting in Louisville.

Back On The Farm

Finally, running out of anything more to say, Mary falls asleep in the corner of the back seat while Becca gets ready to call Ron and let him know we were getting close to the farm. She dials the number and puts the phone on speaker so the Colonel and I could hear.

"Well, good evening. Everything working out okay?" Ron asks, sounding wide awake.

"We're about ten minutes from the farm, so call the SWAT team and tell them we're coming in," Becca declares, now all business.

"Andy and Simone Torres are in Nashville. They'll start for Louisville with Marshalls Donnie Burghardt and Reece Rooney around two o'clock this afternoon. All units will switch to channel six on the radio at noon. The folder with the information we want them to have will be on my desk at eight in the morning. Questions?" Ron directs the operation and sounds on top of everything.

Becca looks at the Colonel and me, "No questions here. We're pulling in the driveway now."

"You guys go get some rest then," and the phone goes dead.

****

Out of the shadows of the oak tree steps an officer armed with an AR-15 and protective vest. He stops our car to check who's aboard. I'm confident there are other officers I couldn't see, but could sense, who were watching our every move. Becca holds her credentials out the window in the beam of the officer's flashlight. He checks the picture, raises the light to her face, then speaks into his radio and motions us forward.

"Where the hell we at?" asks Mary as the flashlight shines in her face interrupting her nap.

"We're at the farm where we're going to stay for a few hours to rest up and wait for the trap to be set," Becca answers, gathering herself together to get out.

I pull the car though the barn door and into the middle between the stalls where we're met by another officer who also checks everyone's ID's. After letting us exit the car, he escorts us to the stairs leading to the apartment as if we'd never been here before. We grab the girl's bags out of the trunk, knowing they'll need something for the night.

"What're you doing here old man, I thought you were retired or died or something," an officer from behind me laughs.

"Just doing this one last job," I answer, turning to see a young officer I had trained awhile back.

"Let me get that for you," he says, reaching for the bag in my hand.

"No, I got this. I want you to keep both your hands free to protect the witness," I reprimand him, thinking he knows better than that.

Once upstairs, I find the Colonel making a pot of coffee and looking for a snack. Looking up, he asks, "You want the recliner or the couch? The girls took the bedroom, and I mean took it like Grant took Richmond."

After looking around the room I can see why the girls took the bedroom. The couch is a love seat, way too short for a bed, with a flower print slipcover so ugly that it alone could keep you awake. The recliner is black leather with the white stuffing peaking out of a tear in the arm and camouflaging a broken spring in the seat.

"You choose, Colonel. I'm thinking about sleeping on the floor, "I answer, eying a thick soft rug under the coffee table.

After a cup of coffee and a ham sandwich, the Colonel turns on the TV and we settle into our resting spots. A look at my watch tells me we got eight hours before we need to get *back in the game*. I can't sleep, thinking about the young officer downstairs, something was not right. I'm uneasy as I go over and over the scene in my head.

Setting The Trap

I wake to Becca standing over me while talking on the radio with Ron, I must have been more tired than I thought. The Colonel is still snoring softly in the recliner.

I can hear Ron saying, "They took the bait. Game on."

"What's going on?" I ask, still trying to get the sandman out of my head.

"Wake up the Colonel and get fresh coffee on. I'll get Mary, I don't want to go over this but once."

Without even opening one eye, the Colonel says, "I'm awake, but put some makeup on so you don't scare people."

"I'll scare you old man, now get that coffee on," Mary orders, appearing in the bedroom door in a large tee shirt and bare feet.

We gather around the serving bar in the kitchen and wait to hear the plan of the day. Becca starts out with, "Ron says the plan is going as designed, someone was in the file this morning. The file had a picture of Simone, which they copied, and they know the name of the hotel and the room number we'll use as the trap. Marshals Burghardt and Rooney will bring Andy and Simone up from Nashville, which is where the report says Mary was staying. Thomas and his team will cover the trip up I65 to the room. They'll be at the hotel at five o'clock, but we'll have Mary there at three. The only real info they have is that Mary is being moved from Nashville. You and the Colonel shower and Mary and I will put lunch together.

"I'm not going to check in a hotel with you guys smelling like you do," Mary grumbles.

"What about you?" the Colonel growls back.

"That's no way for a gentleman to talk to a lady," Becca calls out from the kitchen.

"Who you calling a lady?" he laughs, looking at Mary standing there holding her coffee cup, wearing only a tee shirt and a smile.

"Better yet, who's she calling a gentleman?" Mary snaps back.

"We took a shower while you two were still snoring. So get a shower and put our bags in the car," Becca ends the debate.

I pick up their bags and start to the car after telling the Colonel he could shower first. Once down the steps, the young officer I spoke to when we arrived is still there. Opening the trunk, I throw the bags in and before I can close it, he asks, "You guys moving the witness to the Holiday Inn after lunch?"

"We're kind of in a holding pattern. We may be staying here," I answer and walk back up the stairs.

I call Becca to the bedroom, so we can talk alone. About the time I start to tell her my suspicions and the potential trouble coming our way, the Colonel reminds us from the bathroom that he's trying to take a shower. "Come in here, you need to know this too," I tell him.

"What about her?" the Colonel says, peeking out from behind the door."

"I got three brothers and work with almost all men, you don't have anything that I haven't already seen. Wrap a towel around it and get out here." Becca says, rolling her eyes.

"You ever seen a black man blush?" I ask her.

"What do you guys want?" the Colonel asks, standing far enough from Becca so as not to catch anything.

"The young officer downstairs just asked me if we were going to move the witness to the Holiday Inn. The only way he could have known is by looking in the file on Ron's desk, or talk to somebody that had. Now, we need to talk to Ron and change the plan."

"Hold on, Ray. We knew there was a leak in the feds, but wasn't sure how they were finding out about the security being handled by the police SWAT teams," Becca says, turning her back so the Colonel could get his clothes on.

"So, what are we gonna to do?" the Colonel questions, sitting down close to Becca and appearing more interested in the game plan now, than in her seeing him in his Superman underwear.

"Now that we have a contact for information, we can bait the trap. Let's get started," Becca jumps up off the bed, looks at the Colonel and says, "Put some pants on."

****

Downstairs, I round up the young officer and hand him a cup of coffee.

"How you been doing Danny?" I ask, leaning against the trunk of the car.

"Been great Ray, yourself?" Danny answers, blowing on his coffee.

"Trying to retire but things keep coming up. I told the marshals I'd drive the decoy car on this witness to pick up some golf money."

"Decoy car?" Danny asks, looking down in his cup.

"The witness they tried to kill a couple weeks back was a friend, and she asked for me to be involved. I couldn't be part of the actual protection team, but this is a decoy."

"So we're spending all this time and manpower on a nobody? Where's the real witness?" he asks, acting as if it was his money that was being wasted.

"We'll move this decoy to the hotel, hoping that the bad guys are watching us and not watching the real witness they're moving up I65 from Nashville. We'll need a cop car to accompany us, you want the job?"

Word Games

After talking to the detail boss about using Danny as an escort for the decoy, there was no need to let anyone else in the circle, they had no need to know. We sat Mary down and filled her in on her part of the scam. "Well, that's different, being on this end of the law," Mary shakes her head and smiles, while envisioning playing the part of an agent protecting the 'witness', aka Agent Simone Torres.

"Can you act out the part? It may call for some thinking on the fly," Becca worries.

Wearing jeans that answer the question of how much you can stuff into a five pound bag, a pair of ankle boots with two inch heels and a tight-fitting pullover shirt, Mary puts her hands on her hips with feet wide apart and says with pride, "I've been acting all my life. I walk into a hotel room with a man I've never seen before, ask a question or two and become whatever or whoever he wants me to be. Inside of an hour, I have their money and they have a smile on their face."

"These people will be thinking with their big head, they won't be trying to get you out of your clothes and into bed," the Colonel cautions.

"I understand old man and I can do it!" Mary argues, standing and pointing her finger at the Colonel.

Becca sets her coke can on the table and stands, saying, "Children, here's the way this is gonna play out. Conway will ride in the car with Danny and the Colonel will ride with Mary and me. Ray, where's your shoulder holster?

"In the desk drawer. Why?"

Becca motions towards Mary, saying, "Take the bullets out of the magazine and give it to Mary.

"What're you smoking? I'm not giving my gun to Mary."

"Mary is going to use it as a prop. She'll have it on and make sure that Danny sees it. That'll help sell the fact that she's a marshal, acting as a decoy. Ray, you'll feed info to Danny as we need, and then give him space to move it along," Becca is starting to sound like a real alley cop.

"If we're all ready, I'll go get Danny so we can get this game underway." Standing, I turn toward the stairs.

"Just a minute. Where's the gun you had for the Colonel?" Becca asks.

"In the desk drawer with Ray's. Why?" the Colonel answers.

"Give it to Ray so he'll have a gun. The extra magazines in the shoulder holster will be loaded if you need them. Just follow my lead with Danny," Becca nods for me to go get him.

****

Once Danny and I are at the top of the stairs, we can see everybody standing around the kitchen bar. I almost laugh out loud when I see Mary standing there in my shoulder holster. Stepping forward to shake hands, Becca makes sure I that I don't speak out of turn. "You've met the Colonel and Ray. I'm Becca and for this operation we call this lady Mary. She's the decoy and we don't want to call her by any other name in front of someone not in the circle, so we just call her Mary all the time. You'll be riding with Ray and following us."

"Lets go get your car, Danny, and I'll help you clean out the passenger seat if your car is anything like mine was."

"I'll get my car, it's in the back. I'll put my equipment case in the trunk, that's all I have up there," Danny responds, obviously having girly books or something else in the car he doesn't want me to see.

"Hurry, we need to leave in about an hour so we can get our Mary in room 540 at the Holiday Inn. Then, we can check out rooms 537 and 539 before the witness gets there around five. Danny, you know that the info you hear here is to stay in the group, Ray assures me you can be trusted," Becca warns him as he turns away. Danny nods, then takes the stairs two at a time.

Becca nods, "Good job, Ray."

Jumping back from the bar, Mary knocks over a stool. Then, bending her knees slightly, she leans forward in a TV police stance with her hand on the butt of her gun.

"Let's go get some bad guys," she smiles, causing the mood in the room to lighten considerably.

All Roads Lead To The Holiday Inn

Peering around the corner, I see that the trunk is open and that Danny is on the phone. He's pulled the ugly blue police car in the barn behind Becca's car and changed into a pair of jeans and light blue dress shirt with the tail out to hide his gun. This will work out if I can give him the time and space alone to pass the info along.

"We need to get started," I call out as I round the corner. "The witness is already in Elizabethtown for lunch and they'll be on time. Window of arrival is between five and five thirty," I turn to get my bag to load in the unmarked car that the boss had traded with him.

Danny slams the trunk, "I'll come with you."

Mary is sitting on the bar stool with her legs crossed, looking at Danny as if she was going to pick him up like a john in a bar. I almost feel sorry for him, but he's a big boy. I pick up my bag and head for the car.

"Ray, I'll get that for you. I know you guys got to get ready," Danny offers.

"You can get my bag, Danny," Mary suggests, sliding off the stool.

"Yes ma'am, where's it at?" Danny asks, just like a little boy trying to please his teacher.

As he steps to the bedroom door where Becca is standing just inside talking on the phone, I can see her motion for him to come in. She's telling whoever she's talking to that we'll secure the freight elevator in the garage, so we can move the witness straight to room 539. Danny picks up Mary's bag and hurries to the stairs and out of site. Becca points toward the stairs, cueing me to check on Danny.

I give him a minute to get to the car. Stopping at the bottom of the stairs, I hear him telling the person on the other end what he just heard, so I move back upstairs to tell Becca that we were right about Danny.

Becca, the Colonel, and Mary are standing in a group in the middle of the room looking around, making sure we have everything. Becca asks me if everything is ready and I nod my head 'yes'.

"Well, lets get in the car and go," Mary is now giving orders and moving her shoulder around, trying to adjust to the new weight of the gun as she walks. Anyone paying attention can see she's new to wearing a shoulder holster.

Once everybody is ready to go, Becca waves for me to come over to her car. As I get out of the passenger side door, I tell Danny to stay, "I'll see what she wants now".

"What now, Becca?" I yell, heading her way.

"Get over here so I don't have to yell," Becca bellows.

"Just playing the game for all ears," I say, leaning into the car.

"Give him what he needs to know on the way downtown."

****

The drive to the Holiday Inn takes about thirty minutes, leaving us about two hours to get settled in before the other group arrives.

Once at the hotel, the Colonel pulls their car into the underground garage. Danny walks in with me to check in the hotel and pick up the room keys. We have to sell him that this is the point unit and that the witness is on the way.

Taking the elevator to the fifth floor, we find the hall long, empty and dimly lit. Our assigned rooms are in the middle of the floor, near the snack room. The staff elevator opens in the back of that room and can be watched and controlled from the door off the hall.

Danny and I go to room 539, the one the witness will be using. We open the door and check the room, starting with the closet. We remove the extra blankets from the drawers in the dresser and then lift the mattress up so we can look in the box that's used for a bed frame. Once we're sure the bedroom is safe, we move to the bathroom. We start with the inside of the toilet tank, then check the shower and the cabinet under the sink. We remove all the soap and shampoo and throw the small bottles in a bag to place in the dumpster. I have to make sure that Danny thinks this is for real.

"We checking for cameras and bugs?" Danny asks, starting to look under the lampshade.

"Just checking for bombs. These people don't want to see what she's doing or hear what she's saying, they want to kill her." Danny is sold.

"You watch the door and the room and I'll call Becca to bring up the decoy. Then, I'll get the snack room ready," Danny responds.

Stepping into the snack room, I see Ron leaning against the soft drink machine. He places his finger against his lips, signaling for me to say nothing. Stepping into the hallway and turning toward the rooms, I watch as he walks past 539 to the next room and disappear through the door.

Danny, not knowing him, watches until he hears the door close and then turns back to look at me. We watch the elevator open and the Colonel step off, followed by Becca and Mary. The Colonel steps back to let them pass, then follows them down the hall toward their room. They enter room 539, leaving Danny and myself standing in the hall.

Crossing the hall to room 538, we settle in the room the guys would be using. Once I pick a bed by throwing my stuff on it, I tell Danny I'm going to check on the girls, the witness could be here in about thirty minutes. Danny tells me he's going to use the bathroom and then join us across the hall.

Once I'm in the room and Becca is sure I'm alone, she asks what Danny is doing.

"He says he is using the restroom, but I think he's making a call."

"I believe I've been in this room before," Mary announces, sitting on the corner of the bed and bouncing like a kid.

The Colonel turns back from the window, "What are the odds of that?"

"There are a lot of hotel rooms I haven't been in," Mary snaps, glaring at the Colonel.

"Not in this price range there's not," the Colonel replies, turning back to the window.

"As much fun as this is, you two knock it off," Becca orders, holding her hands up as if parting two children on the playground. Becca's phone rings just as Danny knocks on the door. "All right. We're ready." Returning her phone to her jacket pocket, Becca looks at the group. "Showtime. The witness will be here in about five minutes. Danny, you and Conway go down to the garage and meet the marshals. Mary, you and I will be at the top of the elevator. Colonel, you got the hall and the room."

****

The garage is dark when the marshal's car stops close to the elevator door. I hold the door of the elevator so it can't be called away and Danny moves to the other side of the car to cover any movement in the garage, as Rooney and Burghardt get out of the front seat.

Simone Torres climbs out of the back seat dressed in cut off jeans so short that the pockets hang out, a tee shirt without a bra and her hair in dog ears. Walking up behind

Danny, she pats him on the butt and says, "I'm Mary, what's your name big boy?"

Danny smiles that little boy embarrassed smile and stutters, "I'm Danny and I'm here to help keep you safe, ma'am."

Shaking our heads, Rooney, Burghardt and myself usher the other two onto the elevator and I call Becca to clear the hall, we're coming up.

Once on the floor we move down the hall, pass Ron waiting at the guest elevator with the Colonel and enter room 539. Simone tells everyone she's going to take a shower and would like a little privacy. Turning to Danny, she whispers loudly, "You can stay and watch if you like, cutie."

Ignoring her, Becca says, "I think I'm going to take a shower and change clothes. Which room did you guys take?"

Danny, trying to get as far away from Simone as he can, answers, "We're in room 538."

"Then, I guess we got room 536. I can use a shower too. Shut up Colonel," Mary cuts off his smart mouth before he starts.

"I think Danny, the Colonel and I are going downstairs to get something to eat if you want to go along, Reece."

"I'm going to take a shower, but I'll catch up with you guys in a few."

"I'm going to take a nap, you guys go eat without me," Danny says, opening the door to the hallway and escaping any further attention from Simone.

Once the girls are in their room, we watch Reece disappear into his room and Danny walk to the snack room for a coke.

The Colonel and I duck back in Simone's room and a couple minutes later Ron pops in the door saying, "Danny made a call while he was in the snack room. I think the hit team is close. Stay on your toes."

Sitting in the room with a clock that seems to have stopped, and a 'What? Me worry?' look on our faces, we all turn as Ron's phone rings. After listening, all he says is, "Okay." Returning his phone to his shirt pocket, he walks to the door, looks back in the room and then walks out.

The Mouse Is In The House

Everyone is on the ready to react to anyone attacking the witness. Ron sticks his head back in the partially open door, motioning me out in the hall. After closing the door behind me, Ron walks in the direction of the snack room not saying a word and I follow.

Reece is waiting for us with a man I recognize as Lieutenant Gary Ashby from Internal Affairs.

"What the hell is he doing here?" I ask Reece, ignoring Ashby.

Not giving Reece a chance to answer, Ashby responds, "I'm here to suspend Danny's police powers and would like you there to answer his questions."

"I'm not a fan. Doing this is one of the reasons I never wanted to be in the Rat Squad."

"Lets make this as easy as we can, Ray."

"Easy for who? You?"

Stepping between Gary and me, Ron says, "Lets get this done. You two can have a beer and hurt each other's feelings later."

Entering the room assigned to the guys, we find Danny sitting in a chair at the table watching television. "Danny, I'm here to suspend your police powers," Ashby tells him, holding his hand out for Danny's badge and gun.

"Why?" Danny asks, jumping to his feet and demanding answers, but looking frightened.

"I'm here to take your badge and gun on orders of the Police Chief. Due to the sensitive nature of the case these gentlemen are working on, they'll have to answer your questions," Ashby says, while placing Danny's sidearm in his briefcase and walking out the door.

Ron takes the other chair at the table and motions for Danny to sit down. Never taking his eyes off of me, Danny returns to his chair. Moving closer so that he was looking Danny straight in the eyes, Ron continues, "You will never be a police officer again, but there is a chance you can stay out of jail."

"Why? Exactly why will I not be a policeman and why would I go to jail?"

"You gave information to people that are trying to kill a witness and have already killed a marshall and wounded another," Ron yells, now on his feet and unable to mask his anger.

Now, with a frightened look on his face, Danny says, "I don't know what you're talking about."

Ron, now nose to nose with Danny, snarls, "We're talking about you telling someone what room and hotel that the witness would be staying in. Then, when they miss her the first time, they shot two marshals, killing one and wounding the other. My people, asshole!"

"You guys got it all wrong, I told a buddy at the prosecutor's office how to find Mary Green so he could serve her with some papers. He said the marshals were hiding her so that he couldn't make any money."

"So, you didn't think anything was wrong with that?"

"No, he said this was big money. That Ben Williams had a client that was suing for some big bucks and the feds were hiding her because she was a snitch."

"What else do you know about what's happening today?" Ron asks, seeing that Danny's involvement was more about making a buck than meaning any real harm.

"He told me."

"Who is he?" I ask, not wanting to feel left out.

"John Hart. He serves papers for the attorneys. John told me there would be two men and a woman that would appear as guests and to wait in the hall and serve her when she was out of her room."

"What were you thinking, boy? I taught you better than that."

****

Ron called to update the other agents covering the hotel about what Danny had just told us. The next voice we hear is Detective Tracy Ball, who was on the bus stop in front of the hotel. "There's a group that got out of a rental car in a no parking zone. They're wearing gloves and wiped off everything on the car including door handles, the steering wheel and the trunk where they removed a suitcase. Then, they entered the lobby through a side door."

"This is Basset. They also opened the driver door and threw the keys in the front seat."

Ron speaks into the radio, "Everyone look around and let's find those people. Do not leave your posts, in case we're wrong."

"They just walked by the desk and went up the stairs to the second floor," Basset whispers in the radio.

"Stay with them, but back out of sight. Andy stay with Willy and help cover this group," Ron orders, taking control of what could be an assassination attempt on the witness.

"This is Andy. The lady got on the elevator and the two men took the stairs. Willy, can you take the stairs and I'll try to stay with her."

"Ron, this is Donna. The elevator is stopping on this floor and I'm locking my radio to open mic."

"All detail cars switch to channel three for car to car," Ron says, holding a radio in each hand.

"Ron, this is Willy. The two men are on the landing, outside the fire door on the fifth floor. I'm just below on the fourth floor."

Ron turns, looking at everyone in the room, as from the radio monitoring Donna, we hear a woman say, "Do you have a master key to this floor?"

"Yes ma'am. But if you're locked out of your room, you'll have to go down to the front desk."

"Oh, come on. Don't make me go all the way back down to the front desk. I'm in kind of in a hurry."

"What room do you need in Ma'am?"

"537."

"Ma'am, do you have your check-in paper with you?"

"Just open the door to 537 and do it now."

"Is that a gun, ma'am?"

Everyone in the room is on their feet, guns out, ready for a shoot-out. These are the people that killed a marshal and wounded another and are trying to kill a witness. Glancing around the room, I can see that no one will have a problem extracting a pound of flesh.

"The two men just entered the hallway and I'm moving to the fifth floor door."

"All personnel, cover all entrances to the fifth floor," Ron orders, moving to the door.

Donna's voice erupts from the radio, "Ma'am, here's the key."

"No, you're going with us. Now, open the door to 537."

Ron, speaking into the radio says, "Everyone stand tight and let them commit. Make sure the fifth floor is sealed off, nobody comes or goes."

****

Simone and I move to the bathroom where we turn the hot water on in the shower, filling the room with steam to give the appearance that someone is in the shower, and also to cover any possible reflection in the mirror. Ron takes a spot in a small hang-up closet behind the door and the Colonel lays down behind the far side of the bed just as the door opens.

Two men enter the room with guns at the ready, followed by Donna who is pushed in a chair just past the entrance alcove by the woman, whose gun is also out.

The first man points his gun at Donna and tells the woman to keep an eye on her. His eyes never leave the partially open bathroom door.

As he steps in view of the mirror, we watch as he pushes the door open with the barrel of his gun like a TV gangster. A pro would keep his gun back, close to his body to protect his weapon. I think as I look on that these are not pros, they're cheap back-alley knockoffs. What a time to cut corners.

Pushing the bathroom door open, we can now see his arm and gun through the steam as the door blocks his view of us. Simone grabs the gun and closes her hand over his grip, pulling it down so it's pointing at the man. I hear the bones in his trigger fingers snap as a cry of pain fills the room and freezes everyone in place except Simone, who's flipped the man head down and feet up into the steaming shower water, thereby taking his mind off the pain in his hand.

From the other room, I hear Ron yell, "Drop your guns, it's over!", followed by the Colonel saying, "Yeah, what he said."

Ron opens the hallway door, letting Willy and Andy in as the Colonel peeks through the bathroom door to check on us. With a smile of heartfelt concern he pokes the dripping wet man, curled up in a fetal position holding his burned hand, with the toe of his shoe.

"Damn, that looks like it hurts."

Caught In The Trap

The room was starting to settle down, with the exception of the two grown men acting like babies. The six foot two hundred pound man is crying about needing EMS for his injuries caused by Simone taking his gun, breaking his fingers and throwing his big ass in the hot shower. The other guy is face down on the rug yelling, "Don't tell them anything!"

Andy and Ron are discussing our next steps as I accidently step on the side of the guy's face on the floor, asking him very nicely to stop yelling. I sit him up, rug burn and all, beside the woman. The Colonel drags the crybaby, still holding his hand, over beside them.

Pulling a chair up facing the group, I start explaining how this is going to play out. "We're going to ask you ladies and gentlemen some questions and you will answer."

Motor-mouth interrupts, "We're not telling you pigs shit and you can't make us."

"I'm sorry, maybe I need to clear up some facts. You forced your way into a hotel room being used to house a federal witness with guns drawn, in an attempt to kill a witness. Am I right so far?"

"So what," Crybaby with the broken finger pipes up.

"Well, that's where the story could take a turn. See, you guys can answer our questions and go to the jail, or maybe you could break in where there are marshals and police and a shootout occurs and you all die."

All together they say, "But, there was no shoot out and we weren't shot."

"Ah, but the story's not over yet and we can do whatever we want. Now, here's the catch; y'all have to talk or you have to die."

"Hey, you in charge, you can't just let them kill us," Motor-mouth calls out to Ron.

Ron turns, and looking down at the man says, "I'm sorry, but these two reprobates don't work for me." Then, motioning to Andy, Simone, and Willy to step out in the hallway, he continues, "Lets step out, I think the fewer witnesses the better."

"You can't leave us here with them," the woman cries as the door closes behind Ron and his chosen crew.

The Colonel picks up one of their guns with a silencer and fires a shot in to the headboard, causing pieces of wood to fly in all directions. "If they came charging in the door and we were in the room, one of their shots could have gone there," he says, apparently unconcerned about the tension in the room.

"How about there?" I say, pointing toward the bathroom door, then watching as the Colonel fires a round into it.

The hallway door opens and Andy sticks his head in to ask if everything is all right and to tell us that the lieutenant and the chief are on the way in about half an hour.

As I get my gun out, Motor-mouth looks at me and asks, "What're you planning to do?"

The Colonel answers instead, "We're about to do what my old grandma told us to do on rainy days. We're gonna make our own fun."

"I want you folks to understand that in a shoot-out sometimes people get hit three or four times before they die," I say, pulling the magazine out of my automatic and checking the number of rounds, like I don't already know.

"First time, and maybe the only time; who hired you to waste the witness? We know that you didn't do it for free," I growl, inches from Motor-mouth's face.

"We're not telling you nothing, we're not scared of you," Crybaby says, trying hard to be a bad ass and not cry.

The Colonel fires a shot into the table holding the television causing chunks of plastic to fly in all directions, "Which one of you want to be shot first?"

"Shoot the woman first, but stand her over by the door and get Andy's gun."

The Colonel steps out into the hall and returns with a gun in his hand. Grabbing the woman by the arm and pulling her to her feet, he leads her over by the hallway door. "You think if they got in the room before they knew we were here, she might have tried to hide in this closet?" as he pushes her to the wall.

"Wait. Wait! What do you want to know?"

"Stop. Don't tell them anything, they're not gonna shoot you," bellows Crybaby.

"I'm answering their questions, these two are nuts," the woman whimpers, now in tears.

"So, who hired you guys?" I ask, pulling up a chair and offering it to the woman.

"Williams will kill us," Motor-mouth deplores.

Turning to face the man still sitting on the floor, I ask, "Ben Williams the lawyer?"

"Yes, Ben Williams the lawyer. I didn't want to be a part of it, but they made me. Please don't kill me," the woman begs, barely able to speak.

I step in the hall and ask Simone to come in with the Colonel and then ask her where Ron and Andy are. Simone points at the room next door and advised that the chief and the lieutenant are in there also. I knock, but then just walk in, not waiting for an answer. Danny has been taken to police headquarters, leaving the four men listening to what's taking place in our room.

"We heard, Ray, good job." The chief turns to the others in the room and asks, "Now what?"

Andy, now feeling the power from having a seat at the big table, says offhandedly, "We kill 'em." As everyone turns to stare at him, he follows with, "Well, not really. Just on the news until the trial."

"I'm a little behind the curve so you'll have to draw me a picture," the chief remarks, leaning back against the dressing table.

Andy continues, "Okay, listen up. First, we'll need a trusted cast of players; a homicide team, EMS and a team from ETU. Once everyone has been briefed, we put a call out about a shooting in the hotel. The news will pick it up from the scanner and react. We'll have the marshals take the hit team down the back elevator and house them in a jail out in the state. Then, ETU will take pictures to be used as evidence by the FBI, keeping them out of the reach of the press. Homicide can write up a report, which the captain will see, and he will do what he does best."

"Leak it to the news," I say, not being able to stop myself, but not really trying.

"The defense will make a move to get the charges dropped, and we bring out the witness and start locking people up. I like it kid," the chief says.

Ron, looking back and forth from the kid to the chief, comments, "I think you guys read too many E.E. Kennedy novels."

"I'll make the call and get the players to meet me at the Pancake House on Broadway, nobody will think anything about seeing that group there. Can you get the marshals to move the hit team as soon as possible, Ron?" asks the lieutenant, taking charge.

"Maybe we should question them while they want to talk and haven't asked for a lawyer," I suggest, trying to slow things down before mistakes are made.

Setting The Stage

Once everyone is in agreement that a cast the size of *Gone with the Wind* was not controllable, Ron suggests that we need to separate the hit team in separate rooms, read them their rights and fill out the arrest slips. The chief is going to call the U.S. Attorney and update him on what's going on at the hotel.

This looks like a great time for the Colonel and myself to find Seven Eleven and Big Charlie and get them into the hotel where we can protect them, and above all find them when we need them.

The chief, now off the phone, is in the process of giving Andy and the lieutenant orders. It seems the U.S. Attorney wants the witnesses and all of the prisoners brought to the Federal Court House. Judge Jackson is going to sign arrest warrants and arraign them tonight.

Ron, not wanting to lose control of the case, starts giving assignments, "Simone, you take Mary. Reece, you and

Donna take the woman, and Becca, we'll take the men. Ray, you and the Colonel go get the other witnesses and don't stop for wine."

The Colonel smiles and answers, "We don't need to stop, I got a bottle in the room. But, I could use a dumpster burger."

"Just take them to the parking lot behind the marshals office and someone will meet you there. Leave your guns in the car," the chief orders in the tone that only a police chief uses.

Everyone starts to move at one time, trying to exit the room before the chief is able to get into his overseer roll. The room and hallway is suddenly filled with echoes of, "You get the car" and "I'll meet you at the elevator in the garage".

Once the crowd has all moved to the hall, the chief looks over at the Colonel and myself still standing in the corner smiling."What are you two looking at?" he demands, standing with his hands on his hips and looking like a short Captain Bly.

The Colonel, not being the least bit intimidated, retorts, "I'm not sure, but if someone can tell me what it is, I can tell you what to feed it."

"You two go find those winos and get them to court," a red-faced chief bellows.

"Say pretty please," the Colonel smirks, continuing to poke and insult.

"Get out before I shoot one of you."

Grabbing the Colonel by the arm before he can say anything else, I call over my shoulder, "See you in court."

With the garage being a worm nest of police, marshals, a witness and the three bad guys, the Colonel and I start for our car. We drive by the elevator where the kindergarten class was busy choosing up who would ride with whom and in what car. Turning to look at the Colonel I ask, "Wonder if their mommies know they're playing police?"

****

Finding Big Charlie and Seven Eleven hanging out at the liquor store on Market Street, we wrestle them into the car and head to the Federal Courthouse. Pulling up behind the marshals' office, we stop about three feet from two marshals waiting to show the group to the courtroom. Without asking who we are, they motion for us to move off the lot, official vehicles only. The Colonel tries to tell them we're here to see Judge Jackson, but one of them pulls his coat back showing his badge, and tells us that if we don't move, he'll arrest us and tow our car.

I lean over the Colonel and say, "We're moving officer, have a nice day."

"I'm not an officer, I'm a marshall. Now move before I change my mind."

I move the car to the street and watch as in a few minutes the rest of the gang pulls onto the lot and the marshals show them inside. Ron looks around for us and I move my group of merry men to the front of the courthouse. After taking a seat on the steps, I call Ron who tells me to stay where we are and he'll send someone to get us.

About two seconds later, the door swings open and there stands our favorite marshal.

As I pass by, I say, "Thank you, officer."

"I'm not an officer!"

Without even looking up, the Colonel offers him a dollar saying, "That's right, you're a doorman. Now boy, show us to Judge Jackson's courtroom." Sensing the marshal would like to shoot us, I'm relieved when we safely enter the courtroom.

After instructing Big Charlie and Seven Eleven to take a seat on the back bench, the judge stares down at three public defenders and the U.S. Attorney. The chief and Ron are standing behind the attorneys, with everyone else on the benches on the spectator's side of the bar.

Sliding in, I lean forward between Becca and Simone whispering, "What's going on?"

"The prosecutor is asking the judge to sign the warrants on the hit team and arraign them so their lawyer can set up a deal. Then we can get a statement and they can testify in front of the grand jury," Simone whispers back..

The party in front of the bench breaks up and public defenders take their clients to different parts of the courtroom to bring them up to speed. Ron motions for us to meet him and Owens in the hall, to bring us in out of the dark. We crowd into a conference room; leaving Mary, the two witnesses and the Colonel in the hall.

Closing the door, Owens begins, "I would like to start by clearing the air. You all don't trust me or feel that I'm part of the team, but I know you have a mouthful of questions that you want answers to. So, lets start with my name. I'm Mike Owens, and not whatever colorful adjective you prefix lawyers with. We all have a job to do and it's important that we do it. I need to know right now who's on the team and who's on the bench."

Ron speaks up, "One other thing before you make up your mind. Mike is in charge from this point on and we do not question what he says or what he asks us to do." He looks around, then says, "We're all in, Mike."

"Okay. I'm going to ask the grand jury to indict the hit team for trying to kill a witness and I'm going to get a sealed indictment on Ben Williams. I don't want him to know until the last minute."

Looking him squarely in the eye, Ron asks, "What about the two marshals that got shot? Somebody has to pay for that."

"Come on Ron, we've got to give the hit team a deal that will let them tell us they killed one marshal and wounded another. I'll need you to have Simone, Ray and the Colonel here and ready at nine in the morning and that's the easy job. Becca, you need to have Mary, Seven Eleven, and Big Charlie here at noon. By the way, I'll need to know their real names." From the look on Mike's face and his confident remarks, he feels like he's now a part of the team.

There's a knock on the door and Mary's head appears in the room, "The lawyer wants to talk."

Grand Jury

Ron is up before the rooster, getting everyone on their feet and moving in the direction of the courthouse. I don't know, but would guess, that he'd already talked to Mike a couple of times.

The Colonel rolls over and looking at the clock, complains, "What the hell? It's just 6:30!"

"Ron wants us to get ready for court, I think he's been up all night."

The Colonel continues his complaints, scratching his butt and rubbing his eyes. Clad only in boxer shorts and a tee shirt, he shuffles toward the bathroom just as the hallway door pops open and Simone is standing there dressed in a classy black pants suit and white blouse. With her hair pulled back into a schoolteacher bun, one would almost think she was a lady. That is until she shrieks in her drill instructor voice, "Get it up and get it moving!"

"Don't any of these women knock? I'm going to shower and shave, do I have to wear my suit and tie?" the Colonel grumbles, his brain still on the pillow.

"No, slacks and a dress shirt will be okay. We're just going to meet twelve people not smart enough to get out of jury duty."

The Colonel and I attempt to enjoy our room service waffle with Simone pacing and reminding us to hurry. Then, we're off to court with Simone driving and me praying.

****

The Colonel gets out of the car looking for our personal marshal and Simone turns, telling us both not talk to anyone, break anything or write on the walls. We get off the elevator on the third floor and after a short walk down the hall, Simone stops in front of what appears to be a closet door. Behind the door is a stairwell leading up to a room with chairs sitting in a couple rows like a classroom. From the door of the room, we can see a couple of random pictures taking the place of windows.

Mike Owens enters the room carrying a file with Ron following closely behind. "You've done a good job, Ron. I'm going to get the other three in front of the jury and that'll wrap this part up. I've got one more witness after these three. Simone, you're next."

A short time later, Simone comes out of the jury room and the Colonel goes in. Once Mike steps back inside with the Colonel, I ask her what's going on. She looks around the ten by ten room like she is getting ready to tell a dirty joke. "Mike has a secretary that may be passing information to Ben Williams. He's going to have her in front of the grand jury, hoping that we can tie William's ass to both shootings. Our testimony will cover the attack at the hotel, and Mary, Seven Eleven, and Big Charlie will cover the shooting at the sand pit. When you're done, we need to get back and help Becca get them ready."

"What are their real names, did you hear?" I ask, hoping to get the scoop.

Mike steps out of the jury room door, letting me know it's time for me to testify. The grand jury room is not much different from the one in state court. Mike points for me to take my place behind a table and I take my seat facing two rows of jurors; six on the front row and another six sitting behind them with seats raised, allowing them to see over the heads of those in the front row.

Mike stands up behind a podium and asks me to raise my right hand as the jury foreman swears me in. Then, turning to the foreman, he asks, "If I may, sir?"

Without waiting for an answer, Mike asks me to tell what happened at the hotel and where I was when the hit team forced their way into the room.

At the conclusion of my testimony, Mike asks if the grand jury has any questions or needs any clarification. Not seeing any hands, I stand to leave after thanking the jury for their time.

A voice from the back row stopped me, "Young man, I have a question."

Mike and I both turn to find a grandma-looking lady in a high-collar navy blue dress standing with her hand in the air.

"Yes ma'am," we both answer at the same time.

"Did that cute little lady really kick that big bully's ass?"

"Yes ma'am, she took his gun and flipped him into the bathtub." I answer, my pride in Simone obvious.

Back in the waiting room, I see that the group has grown by nine; the hit team, their lawyers and the marshals who escorted the prisoners from jail. Turning to talk to Mike, I ask him to put the guy from the bathtub on first, the grand jury seems anxious to meet him.

****

Back at the hotel, Becca meets us in the hall as we exit the elevator, still laughing about the little old lady on the grand jury.

"Help me get these two ready, it's like having small children."

"I'll take Seven Eleven. Colonel, you get Big Charlie and you girls can tackle Mary together."

Becca smiles saying, "Oh my God, Mary has been getting ready all morning. She's been in front of the mirror for almost two hours."

"She does know this is the grand jury, not an out call in a hotel room?" the Colonel remarks, walking away to look for Big Charlie.

We agree that giving a big dog a bath in a washtub might have been easier.

Once dressed, the next step was lunch without breaking anything or spilling food on their clothes. Then, we're off to the courthouse.

"I'll ride along to help," I offer.

****

Once we get our two wards settled in the waiting room, we watch as the grand jury returns from lunch and files into the jury room without acknowledging our presence.

In a few minutes, Mike steps in the room and asks for Edward Charles Pennington. Being the only ones there we look about. No one moves.

"Big Charlie, that's you," Mike says, pointing at Charlie.

Once Charlie is out of the room, Becca and I laugh. But not Seven Eleven, he knows he's next.

Shortly, Big Charlie re-enters the waiting room and Mike calls for John James Brady III. This time, even Big Charlie laughs.

"What did they ask you, Charlie?" I ask.

"First, never call me Edward Charles Pennington again. Never. They just asked me about seeing the car and the people down at the sandpit. They wanted to know why we were there and when we found the body under the pizza boxes and about seeing the police. You know, all the things we told you and Andy."

The door from the hallway opens at the same time as Mary exits the jury room. Mary stops as she sees Juan, Pedro, Carlos, their lawyers and the marshals that brought them from the jail. Once everyone was in, Mary comes face to face with the Honorable Benjamin Earl Williams, Esquire.

The Light At The End Of The Tunnel
May Be An Oncoming Train

Williams growls, "Hi", as he passes Mary on the way to take a seat next to Carlos. The uniformed guards stand near the door to the hall, leaving the rest of the room occupied by lawyers in misfitting off the rack suits, all black or gray pin striped, and their clients dressed in faded orange jail jumpsuits.

Grabbing Mary by the arm, Becca leads her out into the hallway, effectively cutting off the verbal exchange that was sure to occur, possibly causing a delay in the trial.

Mike steps into the hall as Becca and I are getting ready to take the group back to the hotel saying, "You all done good. Now, go get some rest and I'll call you when I'm done here."

****

Sitting in the back seat with her lower lip stuck out and arms folded across her chest like my three-year-old granddaughter, Mary stays quiet all the way back. Once there she storms off, mumbling something about me not letting her give Williams a piece of her mind.

Pushing though the group in the hall waiting to welcome the returning heroes, the Colonel cracks when she passes, "Careful, you don't have that many pieces left." Mary shoots him a look that would kill and disappears into her room, slamming the door behind her. Re-appearing a short time later, wearing a pair of pink sweatpants with the word JUICY written across the butt and a low-cut midnight black tee shirt, she grabs Ron and me by our arms and yanks us in the direction of Ron's room, saying "We have to talk."

Leaving the victory party in the hall, Ron asks, "What exactly do we need to talk about?"

"I wasn't sure that Williams was behind trying to kill me until today. I always figured it was Carlos or some of his people, but at court when I looked into his eyes, I knew it was him.

"What makes you think now that Ben Williams would want to kill you?" I ask.

"Because he's the money and the boss behind the drugs and the prostitution, plus he has ties to organized crime," Mary says, walking over to the bar to get a soft drink.

"So why is this the first time I'm hearing about this?" Ron asks, leaning back in his chair.

"Because the DEA guy, Bobby, was so sure he knew everything about the drugs, I didn't tell him anything I didn't have to.

"What do you have to tell us now?" Ron questions, looking for his notebook.

After taking a drink from her coke can, Mary returns to sit on the bed. "It started when Carlos got fired from federal court, Ben said he could make us all a lot of money and keep us out of jail."

Ron's phone interrupts and we hear him say, "Mike, that's great. But, get over here now, things are changing fast."

"Do you want me to wait until the lawyer gets here?" Mary asks.

We both answer, "No!"

"So what happened next?" I ask to get Mary talking again.

"He had Carlos start having the roses shipped in and then sell them to a client of Ben's. Williams showed him how to cook the leaves and then put himself in for ten percent, adding a thousand a month retainer, plus more if he had to go to court."

"What did he do for you and your business, which was already up and running?" I'm now more into the story than building a case.

"He had me get my girls together so he could school them on meeting the police. He said he had a person inside the police department who would know when the vice unit was working and check the names if you called them. He showed us a meter we can put in our purse that'll show if there is a transmitter in the room. He made me the same deal as Carlos; ten percent plus more if he had to go to court with one of my girls."

"That means the money you got out of the storage locker really belonged to Ben Williams, not to Carlos?" I ask, already guessing the answer.

A knock on the door announces Mike's arrival from court, "What's up?"

Ron explains, "We got Williams good and we know why Ben was trying to kill Mary. He's the head guy."

"That gives us the why and how with the hit team and it locks Williams down," Mike is ready for the show to start.

Asking Mary to give us a minute, Mike updates Ron and myself in his overall plan. "The group from the Cook house will be handled in state court, the hit team will plead guilty in Judge Jackson's court to trying to kill a witness and will likely get twenty-five years each. Carlos will be tried for killing one witness and we're asking for the death penalty. Judge Jackson will stop the hearing on the hit team to let us unseal the indictment and take

Williams into custody before calling Carlos's case. We'll have a public defender standing by to take the case."

"I want to be there when they take Williams into custody, it'll be great," I'm now as excited as Ron.

Mike, looking around for a coffee cup, says, "We have to protect all of our witnesses, because if Ben Williams is tied to organized crime, they'll be coming down hard to stop this case. They can't have people testify at any cost."

"I'll call the organized crime unit to see what they know about Williams," Ron worries, pulling his phone from his pocket and walking away toward the window. Five minutes later, he puts his phone back in his pocket commenting, "Well, that didn't take long."

"Well, tell us what they said," Owens is ready to make his case.

"They laughed and said Ben Williams is a 'wanna be ganger'. He's been telling people he has ties, but in real life he's nothing. His wife's family is into numerous big money businesses including banking and they have the money, not Williams."

I point out that may be why the cut rate hit team. Ron and I raise our glasses, toasting that the facts of the case are falling into place.

An Ambush For Williams

The big day is finally here, no more hiding in the hotel with this gang of misfits. The Colonel climbs out of bed to make sure the door is locked. "Sure would like to piss or take a shower without Becca's or Simone's help," the Colonel grouches, heading to the bathroom.

The resounding knock on the door is Ron, making sure we're up. Accepting my fate, I get up and let him in. He steps in to tell us that Mike just called and said we didn't need to go to court, they were just going to arraign Carlos and the hit team and arrest Ben Williams.

The Colonel yells from the bathroom, "No way! Save me a seat, that's what I've been waiting for."

"Make that two," I tell Ron and jump to my feet to scramble into yesterday's clothes.

The Colonel re-appears, already dressed, and grabs his shoes from under the bed.

Once in the hall, we find Becca, Simone, Mary, Big Charlie, Seven Eleven and Ron fidgeting in the hallway.

Mary barks at the Colonel, "It takes you longer to get ready than some girl."

"I wanted to get pretty," the Colonel snaps back.

"Keep wanting," Mary starts for the elevator.

*****

After parking on the back lot of the courthouse, we're met by our favorite marshal, who shows us up the back stairs to the witness waiting room. He instructs us to wait there until the courtroom was open and turns back toward the door.

The Colonel stuck out his hand, and the whole group held their breath as he says, "Good morning and thank you, marshal."

"All right, go on in you guys. You should have good seats, just don't sit in the first two rows," the marshal shakes his head and smiles as he turns his back on us and disappears into the hallway.

Once the judge is ready, the prisoners are all brought in and sat in the jury box so their lawyers can talk to them before their case is called. Carlos and Ben Williams are sitting in a corner by themselves and the hit team is at the other end of the box with their public defenders.

Leaning over, the Colonel whispers, "The orange jump suits against the dark wood make them look like buttercups in the spring."

Ron shushes us like kids in church, telling us to stop talking in court before the judge has us put out.

Judge Jackson asks if everyone is ready and the clerk calls the hit team before the bench. Crybaby looks at his cast, then at Simone and there is no love in his heart.

"You think he wants a re-match?" Mary says in a stage whisper that causes the judge and the clerk to look up.

The judge reads the names and has the clerk read the charges "Your Honor, these defendants are being charged with 18USC 1513, stating that they attempted to murder a witness to prevent them from testifying."

Judge Jackson asks each of the public defenders how their client pleads, and they each plead guilty.

Mike announces to the court that each of the defendants had signed a plea deal and that the state would like thirty days before sentencing. The defendants' lawyers ask that the time in jail count on their sentences.

We can hear Williams telling Carlos, "They will testify against you, but don't worry they can't tie you to those people, and it's going to take more than them saying so to get it done. I'll object to any heresay."

227

As the hit team and their lawyers walk out the door to be returned to jail, a marshal steps in and two more appear at the back door. The judge calls Carlos, and he and Williams step before the bench.

Mike steps forward saying, "Judge, we have some business to take care of before we move forward."

Looking down the row as we all move to the edge of the bench like we are getting ready to kneel in church, Ron exclaims, "This is what we came for."

The two marshals in the back of the room start up the aisle stopping just short of the bar, and the Colonel murmurs, "This is gonna to be better than the circus."

"Your Honor, we have a sealed indictment we need to serve before we go on."

The judge nods and motions for Owens to continue. "The state has an indictment for Mr. Williams and the state feels that his representation of Carlos would be a miscarriage of justice." Two marshals take Ben Williams into custody and the judge motions them forward.

Mary jumps to her feet yelling, "Try to kill me! Now you'll pay."

"Give me back my money, whore," Williams yells back, as the marshals cuff him and then start to lead him away.

Simone and Becca each grab Mary by an arm and pull her back down in her seat as Williams announces he's going to sue everyone and that this is all lies.

Carlos is read the charges against him for killing an informant and making and dealing drugs. He looks over at his new attorney and then pleads not guilty. He's quickly escorted out of the courtroom, all the while glaring at Mary.

Meeting us in the hallway, Mike tells us that everything went well for Andy in state court. "The lawyer for Carlos wants to meet with me. Everyone can go home that has one. Big Charlie and Seven Eleven, let someone at Wayside Mission know where you can be reached. Mary, you'll be going with the marshals. Colonel and Ray, Andy will know how to get ahold of you guys if we need you. The only two trials left are Carlos and Williams and I don't think they're going to want a jury trial. Thank you guys for all the work you've done." He shakes hands with the Colonel and then me. Turning, he strides on down the hallway to his next court appointment.

"You know what sounds good, Ray?" the Colonel asks.

"What?"

"A cup of coffee on the bench, what do you think?"

After saying goodbye to Mary and Simone, who are leaving town to place Mary back in witness protection, we head down Jefferson Street towards the coffee shop, where our favorite college girl was waiting to take our order.

****

Coffee in hand, we cross the street to the bus stop and take a seat on the bench.

"What have you done now, Ray?"

"What are you talking about?"

"Those Ray-Bans dragging those cheap suits down the street have to be feds."

Without removing his sunglasses, the one holding a McDonald's bag confirms that the Colonel was right.

"Which one of you is Ray and which one is the Colonel?" the boy asks, trying to look important.

"Who's asking?"

"Secret Service. The First Lady said we were to find you and give you dumpster burgers and coffee, we bought these by the way, and give you a message."

"Let's have the burgers," the Colonel reaches out, not really caring about any message from the feds.

"What's the message?" I ask.

"The First Lady says to tell you that Martin is doing great, walking with a cane and riding the desk. He and Harris got married and there's going to be a little agent crawling around the White House soon."

****

Laying my head back against the worn plexiglass wall I close my eyes, thinking about all the things that the Colonel and I had been through together since we met on this same bus stop bench, seems a lifetime ago.

"Say mister, you got some change for a coffee?"

Opening my eyes to no Colonel, no Andy and no Secret Service; just a black man in his sixties. Along with the dirt of the street embedded in his clothes, the look in his sad eyes says that he has many stories to tell from the miles he's traveled.

Was it all just a dream?

Standing to give the man some change, from behind me I hear the Colonel complain, "Go to take a piss and right away you start interviewing for my replacement."

Made in the USA
Columbia, SC
05 August 2020

14318613R10128